"I'd be happy to **on weekdays if you want to drop her by."**

Nate smiled again, at once both a charming and disarming gesture. "I'll do that."

No, no, no, no, no! the voice inside of her railed. Not now. Not *this* baby, who reminded her all too much of a similar tiny, smiling infant, one she would never forget.

She had come to Morningway Lodge in part to escape from her memories, not indulge in them with someone else's baby. And though she'd cared for several infants since taking the position here, none had affected her the way Gracie had from the first moment Jessica had seen her.

Her own sweet baby, Elizabeth, had had big brown eyes and curly black hair, as well. Maybe that was it.

Books by Deb Kastner

Love Inspired

A Holiday Prayer
Daddy's Home
Black Hills Bride
The Forgiving Heart
A Daddy at Heart
A Perfect Match
The Christmas Groom
Hart's Harbor
Undercover Blessings
The Heart of a Man
A Wedding in Wyoming
His Texas Bride
The Marine's Baby

DEB KASTNER

lives and writes in colorful Colorado with the Front Range of the Rocky Mountains for inspiration. She loves writing for the Steeple Hill Love Inspired line, where she can write about her two favorite things—faith and love. Her characters range from upbeat and humorous to (her favorite) dark and broody heroes. Her plots fall anywhere in between, from a playful romp to the deeply emotional.

Deb's books have been twice nominated for the *RT Book Reviews* Reviewers' Choice Award for Best Book of the Year for Steeple Hill.

Deb and her husband share their home with their two youngest daughters. Deb is thrilled about the newest member of the family—her first granddaughter, Isabella. What fun to be a granny!

Deb loves to hear from her readers. You can contact her by e-mail at DEBWRTR@aol.com, or on her MySpace or Facebook pages.

The Marine's Baby
Deb Kastner

Steeple
Hill®

Published by Steeple Hill Books™

STEEPLE HILL BOOKS

Steeple
Hill®

Recycling programs
for this product may
not exist in your area.

ISBN-13: 978-0-373-87628-0

THE MARINE'S BABY

For by grace you have been saved through faith, and that not of yourselves; it is the gift of God, not of works, lest anyone should boast.

—*Ephesians* 2:8–9

To Katie. You have the kindest heart *ever,* and I have so much to learn from you. I'm so proud of the young woman my "baby" girl has become. I love you more every day.

Chapter One

The baby, sleeping soundly with her tiny thumb pressed in her mouth and her index finger crooked over her button nose, was cooperating beautifully.

The car seat, not so much.

Sergeant First Class Nathan Morningway scowled at the offensive piece of equipment and grunted as he tried the release lever again. At least he *thought* it was the release lever. The directions enclosed in the box had been less than helpful, and he'd chosen to wing it instead. He now wished he'd at least *kept* the useless instructions instead of wadding them up and tossing them in the nearest garbage can.

How hard could this be?

As a marine, he'd taken apart and reassembled countless firearms. He'd defused hundreds of bombs and improvised explosive devices over the years. And he couldn't handle a simple baby seat?

Nate tried the lever once more, and then decided it wasn't worth the effort. He'd just have to figure out how to use the uncooperative piece of equipment after he'd spoken to his brother.

Instead, he unhooked the straps, intending to take baby Gracie out of the car seat and carry her in his arms. The only problem was—and Nate hadn't noticed this until he'd already unbuckled the harness—Gracie's arm was wrapped like a noose around one of the straps, anchored by the thumb she was sucking.

Oh, boy. He really hated to do this, but he didn't see any other way around it. Holding his breath, he gently pulled on Gracie's little fist. She made a small murmur of protest and sucked even harder.

Nate tried again, more firmly this time. Gracie's thumb left her mouth with a pop. The baby's enormous brown eyes opened and blinked back at him. Her chin started quivering, her face scrunched up adorably and a moment later she was howling at the top of her lungs.

Nate grimaced. He still couldn't believe something *that small* could make so much noise. He'd never been around babies before in his entire life.

And now…

Now.

His throat tightened and burned as he fought to suppress the memories. He had to concentrate on other issues right now, the most pressing of which was letting his brother, Vince, know he was back at the lodge. That was enough to worry about all by itself.

"All right, little one," Nate soothed, pulling the pink-clad infant awkwardly to his chest. "I'm here for you. Don't cry, sweetheart."

Nate was surprised when the baby instantly calmed to his voice, curling into his chest and gurgling contentedly. He got a whiff of her soft downy hair and the unique smell of baby shampoo, and his heart flipped right over. Little Gracie had him wrapped around her tiny pinky finger, and there was no denying it.

Gracie wasn't just his responsibility—she was the love of his life. From the moment he'd signed the legal documents that made him not only her godfather, but her legal guardian, Nate had fallen hard for the little one hook, line and sinker.

Too bad he didn't know the first thing about raising an infant. That would be problematic, but Nate had more immediate concerns—showing up at Morningway Lodge unannounced.

His parents'—his *father's*—dream, and now his brother's ministry, the lodge was an affordable retreat center for families of those recuperating from spinal injuries at the nearby Rocky Mountain Rehabilitation Hospital. The lodge was his family's business, and Nate's worst nightmare.

Or rather, his brother *Vince* was Nate's worst nightmare. He had been in the past, and in all probability, he would be again now.

There was only one way to find out, and Nate had never been a procrastinator.

Kissing his baby girl on her soft cheek, he tucked his palm beneath her head and marched up the stairs onto the pinewood porch of the main lodge. He inhaled deeply of the fragrant wood as he let himself in the front door and moved up to the courtesy desk. It was the scent of home and his childhood.

It felt odd to be back home.

Since no one was manning the desk, Nate shifted Gracie securely into one arm and rang for service. He waited a moment, and then, when no one appeared, he bounced his palm several times on the bell.

"I'm sorry to keep you waiting." A young woman whirled into the office behind the desk, brushing her shoulder-length wavy blond hair from her forehead with the tips of her fingers. "Oh, what a darling little baby girl!"

When the woman met his gaze, Nate's breath stopped short in his throat. She had the most luminous chocolate-brown eyes he'd ever seen, and they were openly friendly.

More than that. Brimming with joy. He thought the look in her eyes exactly matched her spacious, heart-stealing smile.

How could anyone be truly happy working as a clerk at Morningway Lodge? Despite the fact that he was glad to be coming back home at last, Nate couldn't think of anything he'd rather *not* do other than work here. Tucked inside the foothills of the great Rocky Mountains, this place was officially the middle of nowhere.

Nate had always been a social person and loved being part of a crowd. It had been that way since he was a small boy.

He couldn't imagine spending his whole life working in such an isolated area. Coming home to the lodge now was a temporary solution to his immediate problem, until he could work out something more permanent—and more agreeable to his outgoing nature. If it weren't for his father's possibly life-threatening stroke, Nate wouldn't be here at the lodge at all.

Anywhere was better than this.

He glanced down at the baby, who was wiggling in his arms and babbling sweet, nonsense syllables that reminded Nate of the call of a dove. Gracie leaned her whole tiny frame toward the woman behind the desk, her arms outstretched to the lady. To Nate's surprise, the baby was smiling—the first time he could remember seeing Gracie smile since her parents had passed.

He swallowed past the lump in his throat. Gracie certainly never smiled at *him* that way.

Nate wrapped his other arm around the baby and pulled her close to his shoulder, feeling oddly possessive of the still-wiggling infant, who protested audibly at his restrictive action.

The clerk had, perhaps instinctively, reached toward the baby, but when Nate adjusted Gracie onto his shoulder, the woman dropped her arms, choosing instead to reach for a large date book on the counter and flip through the pages to the appropriate date.

"What name is your reservation under?" she queried in a soft, sweet voice that matched her looks exactly.

"I—er—don't have a reservation," Nate stammered, thrown off by her question.

The woman's smile wavered. "Oh, I'm sorry, sir. We don't take walk-ins. Do you have someone staying at the physical rehab center? I can put your name on our waiting list. I know it's around here somewhere." She fumbled around the desk, rifling through piles of papers in search of the elusive file. "I'm sorry if I appear disorganized. I don't usually run the desk."

"That's okay, ma'am. I'm just here to see Vince," Nate informed her. "Could you get him for me?"

"I'm sorry, sir," she apologized again. "Mr. Morningway asked not to be disturbed. Would you like to leave him a message?"

Mr. Morningway?

Nate frowned and shook his head to dislodge the uncomfortable image which had formed there, the caricature melding of his pop's and brother's faces. His brother was getting formal in his *old age,* two years older than Nate's own twenty-eight years.

"He'll want to see me," Nate insisted.

The woman glanced uncertainly over her shoulder toward the back office.

Smiling inwardly, Nate was about to give his name when a harried-looking Vince slipped behind the booth, pushing his rectangular glasses up on his nose and then scrubbing a hand through his already ruffled hair. A surprising thatch of gray fell across his forehead, a shockingly light streak through his otherwise dark brown hair.

"Is there a problem out here?" Vince queried the woman before he spotted Nate.

Nate could tell the very moment his elder brother saw him, as Vince's face creased into a frown, his brow furrowed. Nate smiled, but Vince only grunted and continued to glower.

"Hello, brother," Nate said, ignoring Vince's sour-lipped expression.

"Nate," Vince replied, his blue eyes narrowing and shifting between Nate and little Gracie.

Leaning close to the baby to inhale her sweet, unique and somehow calming scent, Nate fidgeted, waiting for Vince to take the lead. Even after all these years away from the lodge and his brother, Vince somehow unsettled him, which only served to annoy Nate more.

The good son glowering at the black sheep of the family. Nate couldn't help but think this whole idea was a gigantic mistake and wondered for the hundredth time why he had decided to come.

"What are you doing here?" Vince asked after a long pause. His voice was a severe monotone that Nate remembered well.

"This is my home, too," Nate reminded him gruffly, though that wasn't completely true.

Morningway Lodge *had* been his childhood home, but he'd been gone for nearly ten years now. And here he stood, lingering at the front desk like a regular patron. It was hardly the same thing.

"*Your* home?" the woman standing next to Vince echoed, her voice laced with surprise. "You never told me you had a brother, Vince."

"This *was* your home, Nate," Vince said, glancing between Nate and the woman at his side and shrugging apologetically to her before turning his gaze back on Nate. "You left, remember?"

Nate did remember. And he hadn't regretted it for a single moment. He had his reasons for leaving, and Vince of all people knew what they were.

"Jessica, this is my brother, Nate. Nate, Jessica," Vince offered curtly, almost as an afterthought.

Nate nodded at Jessica, wishing the woman wasn't present to hear this interchange between him and his brother. It was humiliating.

Grasping in desperation, Nate switched tactics. He didn't want to argue with Vince, especially in front of a woman who was nothing more than a stranger to him. "Don't you want to meet your new niece?"

Vince's expression instantly went from angry to astonished, his eyes widening to enormous proportions as he looked at the baby with new eyes. His mouth opened and closed several times without sound.

"My what?" Vince squeaked, his voice a good octave over its usual deep tone.

Nate chuckled. He hadn't planned to spring this news on his brother in quite this way, but it was worth it just to see the look on his face. "Your niece. Vince, this is Gracie."

"I didn't know you had a child," Vince grated, but he reached out a tentative finger, which Gracie promptly clasped and pulled toward her mouth. Vince smiled at the baby.

"She's not mine," Nate amended. "I mean, she's mine. But she's not *mine*."

Vince's eyebrow shot up in surprise. He reached for Gracie, softly cooing to her. Nate was surprised at how easily and naturally Vince held little Gracie. Nate always felt like a big, uncoordinated gorilla with the baby in his arms.

He shrugged as emotion welled in his throat. Explaining the situation to Vince was going to be the most difficult part of an entirely excruciating exchange.

"Hi there," Vince said, directing his words to the baby. "I'm your uncle Vince. I'm afraid your daddy didn't tell me anything about you."

Daddy. Nate wasn't sure he was ready for that word yet—or if he ever would be.

"Like I said, she's not mine. She is my friend Ezra's daughter. Ezra was my battle buddy in the marines— and my best friend. He had my back in Iraq. I would be dead a dozen times over if it wasn't for him."

Nate paused when his voice cracked. Shaking his

head, he cleared his throat and tried again. "When Gracie was born, Ezra and his wife, Tamyra, asked me to be Gracie's godfather. Two weeks ago, Ezra and Tamyra were involved in a fatal car accident. Tamyra died on the scene. Ezra was in critical condition for twenty-four hours before he passed."

Vince frowned, his blue eyes surprisingly empathetic. "I'm sorry to hear it."

When Nate didn't immediately continue his story, Vince pinched his lips together for a moment, debating, Nate thought, on whether or not to ask the question that was obviously plaguing him. "I still don't understand. Why do *you* have Gracie?"

"I was at Ezra's side when he passed on," Nate explained tightly, absently brushing Gracie's dark, curly hair back from her forehead. He felt the need to touch the baby even as Vince continued to hold her. "Ezra was an only child, as was Tamyra. He..." he swallowed hard "...asked me to raise her."

Vince whistled low and shook his head.

"Wow. That's quite a story." He kissed Gracie's forehead. "But I have to ask—why didn't you just tell him you wouldn't do it? I'm sure you'll agree you aren't exactly father material, Nate."

The woman laid a hand on Vince's forearm as if to restrain him. Her gaze darted to Nate before she flashed Vince a cautionary warning glance.

A nice gesture, Nate thought sardonically, but decades too late.

He glared at Vince. Nate privately agreed with his brother's assessment of his character, but he still didn't like it that Vince had voiced his opinion aloud, especially with a beautiful, smiling stranger present.

Besides, the man Nate was now didn't even remotely resemble the boy who'd run off and joined the U.S. Marines ten years ago. It took him a moment to collect his thoughts enough to voice them.

He could argue, but really, what was the point? Vince wasn't going to change his mind.

"Be that as it may," Nate growled at last, "it was Ezra's dying wish that I take Gracie's guardianship. They even wrote me into their will. To be honest, I'm not sure there were any other living relatives who could take Gracie. The bottom line is that I made Ezra a promise, and I'm not going to go back on it."

Vince scoffed and shook his head again. "That would be a first."

"Vince," Nate warned with a hiss, his eyes narrowing. "Lay off."

How dare his brother question his honor? Nate was a marine now. Or at least he had been. He'd been honorably discharged at the end of his last tour of duty in order to take care of Gracie. It had been his own decision. The life of a military single father wasn't what he wanted for the baby girl.

Besides, he didn't know how he would be able to properly care for Gracie if he was gone all the time. He finally had the time and opportunity to return to his childhood home and see his ailing father, and at the time, it had seemed the right thing to do.

Now he doubted his own wisdom.

His father no doubt expected the worst from him, and would not care one way or the other whether Nate showed up. Why was he trying so hard?

Because, he mentally amended, answering his own question, it was the right thing to do. And Nate respected himself, even if his family didn't extend him the same courtesy.

Nate eyed Jessica's hand, which was still on Vince's forearm. Maybe the best thing to do was just change the subject.

"Did you get married and forget to send me the invitation?"

Jessica colored brightly and withdrew her hand from Vince's arm as if she'd touched a burning stove top. Nate couldn't help but chuckle at the mortified expression on her face.

Vince just rolled his eyes and snorted.

"Hardly. When would I have had time to get married? I can't even make time to date. You left me to take care of everything around here, remember? I didn't have the luxury of doing whatever I wanted with my life the way you did, bro. I still don't." Bitterness rolled off of every syllable.

Nate clenched his fist. So Vince viewed him as a problem already, did he? Why was Nate surprised? He surreptitiously glanced at his watch. He had only been here for five minutes.

Vince hadn't changed one bit since Nate had left all those years ago.

Nothing had changed.

Chapter Two

Nate wanted to punch the sneer right off his brother's face, but he restrained himself, with effort. Maybe later, when Jessica wasn't there to watch.

Vince smiled at Jessica and shrugged an unspoken apology to her, and then slipped the suddenly fussy baby into her arms.

Nate would normally have felt a bit uncomfortable with a stranger holding the baby, but he observed the natural way the woman cuddled Gracie to her shoulder and wished he had some of whatever instinct it was that made some people so easy around babies.

The woman closed her eyes and tucked her chin close to Gracie's curly head. Jessica smiled, and then frowned, and then smiled again.

What was up with that?

"Jessica runs the day care center down the road," Vince explained with a wave of his hand, as if he were brushing off the question Nate hadn't even thought to ask. "You'll no doubt need some assistance with Gracie here, and no one knows children better than Jessica Sabin."

Nate opened his mouth to argue and then closed it again. His gaze slid back to the pretty blond-haired woman at Vince's side, who was now cuddling baby Gracie in the curve of her arm and murmuring in pleasant undertones. Nate was hesitant to admit Vince might be right, but the way the pretty woman immediately calmed the fussy baby did much to persuade him.

There was no denying it. He *did* need help with Gracie. That was a fact.

"Thanks," he said at last, casting Jess half a grin. "I appreciate the offer."

Vince nodded, looking pleased with himself. "Do you want me to go get Pop? I'm sure he'll want to know you're home. And I know he'll want to meet the baby."

Nate shook his head fiercely. He knew he had to face his father sooner or later, but he was definitely leaning toward *later*. He was under enough stress without confronting Pop.

"No. I don't want him to know I'm here, Vince. At least, not yet."

When Nate saw his father again, he wanted it to be on his own terms. In his own good time.

He leveled his gaze on his brother. "Promise me you won't say anything to him."

Vince arched his eyebrow and shrugged. "Whatever floats your boat. I won't say anything. But you need to go see him. When you're ready."

Nate scowled at his brother. All his life, Vince had ordered him around. Why had he expected things to be different now?

He sighed inwardly. He hadn't really expected change, and that saddened him more than anything.

"Where are you staying, again?" Vince asked in what Nate thought was an overt attempt to steer the subject to more neutral ground.

Nate shrugged and grimaced.

"I didn't say," he murmured. "Here at the lodge, I hope. Unless, of course, that's an inconvenience to you."

Nate thought the look on Vince's face was clear affirmation that Nate was, in fact, a considerable inconvenience to his elder brother, but Vince's soft words belied his expression. "As you pointed out, this is your home. You are always welcome here. Your old cabin is still waiting for you."

Vince hadn't rented out Nate's old cabin?

That came as an overwhelming surprise to him. Desperate to affirm his independence, Nate had moved into his own cabin and away from the family quarters in the lodge on his sixteenth birthday. He'd selfishly not cared how his family felt about it. Yet Vince had kept the cabin intact and waiting for him, at his own loss, for Nate knew Vince could have been cashing in by renting the cabin out to guests.

Yet he hadn't. Why?

He shook his head. Not wanting to think too much on what that might mean, he turned his attention to the smiling woman by Vince's side.

"Jess," Nate offered, nodding his head toward the woman and reaching his hands out for Gracie. He suddenly and inexplicably wanted the infant back in his arms, even if it felt awkward, and probably looked worse. "I can take the baby now."

"It's Jessica," she corrected, only briefly glancing at Nate before her gaze returned to the baby, whom she didn't immediately relinquish. "What can I do to help?"

"Not a thing, ma'am," Nate snapped impatiently, then winced at his own harsh tone. With Vince glowering at him, he felt as if he was on trial, and all because, as Vince had said, Nate wasn't exactly *daddy material*.

But he would learn to be. And quickly. He was nothing if not determined.

"Sorry," he apologized gruffly, but that didn't stop him from scooping Gracie back into his arms. He kissed the baby's soft cheek, wishing she would smile at him as she did at Jess.

It didn't seem fair to Nate that Gracie started squirming and protesting the moment she was back in his arms, squawking and reaching out for a woman she had only just met, rather than wanting to be in her own guardian's arms.

Not that Nate could blame her.

Jess shrugged. "No problem."

"Thank you, anyway," he continued, trying to take the edge off his earlier tone, "but I'm sure Gracie and I will get along just fine on our own, at least for right now. We'll see how it goes."

Vince barked out a laugh and shook his head in disbelief.

"Oh, right, little brother. You have been taking care of babies all your life."

"Well, no, but…"

"You *do* know she needs a diaper change?" Jess asked, arching one golden eyebrow and grinning wryly. Nate might have taken offense, but her large brown eyes radiated kindness.

"I—er, well of course I know," Nate said, patting Gracie on her plump behind.

In truth, he hadn't noticed until Jess brought it to his attention. What Nate knew about babies could fit onto the head of a pin.

That was one problem he was going to have to fix, and fast.

"Would you like me to change her for you?" Jess asked with a polite smile. Her gaze was steeped in amusement, but Nate couldn't argue. A rough-cut marine holding a tiny baby girl had to look fairly humorous to anyone's eyes, especially to this day care director, who no doubt took care of babies every day.

He shook his head before he could think better of it. "I've got it. Thanks."

"You're sure?" Jess queried.

Nate shook his head again. "I'll just go over—" He hesitated, looking around the lodge's day room. No thought presented itself that would reasonably complete his sentence, so he let it dangle as awkwardly as the baby squirming in his arms.

"The sofa, perhaps?" she suggested. This time Nate was certain he heard a little teasing in her tone, not that he could blame her.

"Right. The couch." He moved toward the sofa as he spoke, not wanting to make eye contact with either Jess or Vince.

"Do you have a changing pad?" Jess asked from directly behind his left shoulder.

Nate couldn't remember what he had in the diaper bag, but by the weight of it, he was positive he'd packed everything, including the kitchen sink. He'd certainly cleaned out the infant shelves of the baby store where he'd stopped to pick up necessary baby items on his trip to Colorado.

Settling himself on the couch, Nate propped Gracie on his knee and reached for the diaper bag.

Changing pad. Changing pad.

What did a changing pad look like?

Chuckling, Jess seated herself next to Nate. "Here you go," she said, pointing to a folded piece of vinyl.

When Nate didn't move fast enough, Jess snatched up the changing pad and unfolded it on the surface of the couch, then gently removed Gracie from Nate's arm and arranged her on the surface.

"Diaper?" she queried, lifting an open palm.

Nate knew what *that* was, anyway. He handed her a fresh diaper and the box of wipes he'd purchased.

He belatedly realized he was allowing the woman to take over, but he brushed it off, knowing it would be useful to watch an expert change Gracie's diaper for once, and certainly the baby would appreciate it. His own attempts to change the infant during the drive to Colorado were questionable at best, to which Gracie's current saggy baggies attested.

And he hadn't even known about the changing pad. He'd just changed her on a blanket.

Jess had Gracie's diaper off in moments, despite how the baby girl wiggled and kicked. Her soft, sweet voice affected Nate more than he cared to admit, so it wasn't any surprise to him that Gracie responded with happy smiles and coos.

He just wished the baby girl would respond to *him* that way.

* * *

"Oh, you poor little thing," Jessica told the wriggling infant, before glancing back at Nate. He might be considered handsome in a rough-cut sort of way, with his military-short light brown hair and gold-flecked eyes, but he obviously knew nothing about taking care of a baby.

"What?" Nate queried. Jessica thought he sounded slightly defensive, and that, for some reason, embarrassed her. She felt her face warm under his intense gaze, hating that she was so easily ruffled.

"Gracie has a diaper rash." She tried not to make it sound like an accusation, but thought it probably sounded like one, regardless. Her face went from warm to burning hot, and she was concerned that her countenance would reflect how she was feeling inside. She had to be as red as a cherry.

Pursing her lips, she deliberately softened her next words. "Do you have any ointment?"

"Ointment," Nate repeated, digging haplessly through the diaper bag. "What exactly am I looking for?"

"A tube, like toothpaste," Jessica said with a laugh. Now that she wasn't the only one flustered, she could relax about it.

Nate continued his search, but to no avail. After a moment he gave up rummaging and shrugged at her.

"I don't think I have any," he admitted at wryly. He flashed Jessica a rueful grin. "I'm afraid I'm not as armed and organized as I need to be. I didn't know what Gracie would need, so I thought I bought a little bit of everything I could find. Obviously I missed something."

"Babies require a lot of gear," Jessica informed him, efficiently wrapping Gracie in a clean diaper with the ease of experience. "I'd be happy to go into Boulder with you tomorrow to help you stock up on basic supplies."

Nate flashed her a lopsided smile. He *was* a handsome man, she thought again. If she were looking for that sort of thing.

Which she definitely wasn't.

She wasn't looking for any kind of man at all—now or ever. Military men included, even if they looked ridiculously heartwarming and adorable as they toted around cute little baby girls.

Especially if they toted around cute little baby girls. Even the thought choked her up emotionally, and she was immediately on the defensive.

"In the meantime," she suggested, refusing to dwell on the past and reluctantly turning her mind back to the problem at hand, "we need to do something for Gracie's rash. I think I have some petroleum jelly back at my cabin. That will do in a pinch."

"Petroleum jelly? I would never have thought of that," he admitted with a low whistle and a shake of his head. "I'm definitely a newbie."

He laughed, obviously comfortable enough with himself to smile at his own weaknesses. Jessica admired that, and wished her own personality was more like that. "And there are no doubt many things I haven't thought of, where a baby is concerned. Like what I'm going to do with her while I am out looking for a job, for starters."

"We have an opening at the day care," Jessica replied, jumping in more quickly than she should have.

She had her reasons for being hesitant, yet her mouth opened before her brain had a chance to get in edgewise. But as it was too late to take back the words, she continued.

"I'd be happy to care for Gracie on weekdays if you want to drop her by."

Nate smiled again, at once both a charming and disarming gesture. "I'll do that."

No, no, no, no, no! the voice inside of her railed. Not now.

Not *this* baby, who reminded her all too much of a similar tiny, smiling infant; one little baby she would never forget.

She had come to Morningway Lodge in part to escape from her memories, not indulge them with someone else's baby. And though she'd cared for several infants since taking the position here, none had affected her the way Gracie had, from the first moment Jessica had seen her.

The memories were still far too painfully fresh and easily goaded to the forefront of her mind. Her own sweet baby, Elizabeth, had had big brown eyes and curly black hair, as well. Maybe that was it.

Maybe it was that the children in her day care, who belonged to the families who resided at Morningway Lodge while their loved ones recuperated at the nearby physical rehabilitation hospital, never stayed around for more than a few months.

It was safe, relatively, not to get emotionally involved. But Nate—and Gracie—were Morningways. They could be around forever.

By offering to help Nate Morningway, she realized with a sharp stab of pain to her heart, she had potentially just become her own worst enemy.

Chapter Three

Nate never appeared.

Jessica stared out the large bay window overlooking the front side of the day care and sighed. Absently she noted the long shadows of the pine trees that signaled that the sun would soon be setting.

Friday afternoon, and not a word from Nate, other than the time he'd called—at the last minute—and canceled their trip to the baby store in Boulder. In the week since, he'd not once brought Gracie by the day care. In point of fact, Jessica hadn't seen Nate—or Gracie—at all. Not even in passing.

She didn't know why it bothered her, but it did nonetheless.

Actually, she knew *exactly* why it bothered her.

Gracie.

That little baby girl had captured Jessica's heart the moment Nate had walked into the lodge with her in his arms. What a sweetheart.

Melancholy drifted over her like a black storm cloud and burst into rain, flooding through her heart and leaving her limbs weak.

Jessica couldn't deny the fact that Gracie reminded her of Elizabeth. There wasn't a single day that went by that Jessica didn't think of Elizabeth and weep, not in two years. Every single day and night since eight-month-old Elizabeth's unexpected death from SIDS, Jessica's arms and heart had painfully ached for the child.

That was why, she supposed, that as much as it had hurt, holding Gracie had been such a blessing. Babies were God's special gift, even those that only stayed on this earth a short while.

And there was just *something* about Gracie, something special that set her apart. Something that felt different than her experiences with the other babies she'd cared for since she'd taken the position as director of the day care at Morningway Lodge nearly a year earlier.

Why hadn't Nate brought Gracie by?

For better—or more likely for worse—Jessica had looked forward to interacting with the sweet baby girl every day at the day care.

Well, she realized as she finished putting toys back in the bin and surveying the empty toddler room at the day care, there was one way to find out. She would swing by Nate's cabin on her way home from work and find out what was keeping the man. And if she got to spend a little time with Gracie, that was a plus.

After locking up, she headed straight to Nate's cabin, walking quickly and with purpose. She didn't want to give herself time to talk herself out of it, and maybe never see the baby again.

Gah! she thought as she finally stood on the doorstep of Nate's cabin. This was awkward, especially for a self-proclaimed introvert like Jessica.

She could definitely be accused of being a worrywort. But a busybody? Not so much.

Given the pros and cons of her current actions, the list was hardly equal. There were more than enough reasons for her to turn herself around right now and walk away. No harm done, right?

With a quiet murmur and a shake of her head, Jessica raised her hand and knocked on the screen door. Gracie might need her, she reminded herself.

The baby *probably* needed her, with only an inexperienced and obviously proud-to-a-fault marine taking care of her.

The door behind the screen was open. When no one immediately answered her knock, Jessica cupped her hand to her forehead to block the glare of the evening sunshine and peered inside.

"Hello? Mr. Morningway?" she called softly, her heart loudly humming in her ears. "It's Jessica Sabin from the day care."

"Door is open, Jess," called Nate's coarse, disembodied voice. "In the kitchen. And please. It's Nate. Mr. Morningway is my pop—or my brother."

Jessica let herself in, fighting herself every step of the way. This was so far out of her comfort zone it wasn't even funny, but she wouldn't let that stop her. It wasn't the first time, and she was certain it wouldn't be the last, though it didn't help that Nate was such an incredibly handsome man.

Okay, that was enough of that kind of thinking. She was going to talk herself out of this yet.

"Ay-uh, ay-uh, ay-uh," Gracie screeched when

Jessica entered the kitchen. She banged her fists repeat-edly on the tray in a staccato rhythm.

The baby was seated in her high chair and facing the door. Nate sat with his back to Jessica, an infant spoon in one hand and a jar of pureed carrots in the other. He didn't look around when she entered the kitchen, his gaze solely focused on his infant ward.

"One more bite," he coaxed, holding the spoon to Gracie's tiny mouth. "Come on now, girl. Open wide and say ah."

"Ah, ah," Gracie complied, giving Jessica a wide, toothless grin. She flapped her arms wildly and banged her little fists on the high chair with excited abandon. Jessica had never felt so welcome as she did from the baby's innocent greeting.

"Well, she's glad to see *you*," Nate commented, sounding at once amused and annoyed. Taking advan-tage of Gracie's open mouth, he slipped a spoonful of carrots between her lips.

"Ah-bbbb," said baby Gracie.

"Ack!" exclaimed Nate as Gracie's enthusiastic raspberry covered his olive-green T-shirt with orange spots.

Jessica couldn't help the laughter that bubbled from her chest.

"Sure, sure. Feel free to laugh." Nate shot Jessica a faux glare across his shoulder, his features crinkled in distaste but a wry, self-deprecating grin on his lips that belied his tone.

Jessica clapped a hand over her mouth, but not before another giggle escaped.

"I'm sorry," she apologized, her shoulders heaving

from the hopeless effort of restraining her laughter. "It's just that you look so—"

"Foolish?" he offered, joining his own laughter with hers.

She was going to say *cute,* she realized, feeling a blush rise to her cheeks. And just how would that have sounded?

To cover her own embarrassment, Jessica reached for the baby wipes on the table and methodically scrubbed Gracie's face and hands before lifting the infant from the chair and into her arms.

"Feeding this baby is *way* harder than it looks," Nate observed wryly. "I'd rather face an IED."

"IED?" Jessica queried. Leaning in close to Gracie's cheek, Jessica inhaled deeply. She could never quite get enough of the just-bathed lotion smell that was distinctive to babies.

"Improvised explosive device," Nate clarified. "A homemade bomb."

"You defused bombs in the marines?"

"That was my specialty. I suspect it doesn't translate well into civilian life, though. One thing I know for certain—my training is of absolutely no use in learning to take care of Gracie."

Jessica chuckled softly. "No, I don't suppose it is. I'll pray for you, though."

"I—er—just let me go change my shirt real quick," Nate said before beelining it straight out of the kitchen. "I'll only be a moment," he tossed over his shoulder as he went.

Jessica didn't miss Nate's discomfort at her mention of prayer, but her faith was an intricate part of who she was. God had pulled her out of the mire of her own desperation, and she couldn't help but be vocal about her love for Christ now.

She wondered about Nate's faith—or lack thereof. His brother, Vince, was a committed Christian.

None of your business, she reminded herself once again, frowning.

Still, she didn't mind the opportunity to regain her equilibrium that Nate's quick exit had afforded her. She was grateful for a moment to step back and catch her breath, emotionally speaking.

She could be in deep water here. Mentally, she acknowledged her physical attraction to Nate and recognized it for what it was, and then determined within herself to let it go.

As long as she didn't dwell on it, there was no harm, no foul, she told herself resolutely. There was *no way* she was going to submit herself to heartbreak again in this lifetime.

Anyway, the only reason that Nate appeared so adorable to Jessica was his association with baby Gracie. Or at least that was what she was going to keep telling herself. Over and over again, if necessary.

Jessica turned her attention to Gracie, noting that she wasn't the only one to appear flushed—Gracie's cheeks were a rosy red. Alarms blared in Jessica's head and her heartbeat picked up tempo as she pressed the back side of her fingers to the baby's warm face.

"Nate?" she called hesitantly.

"Yep?" he replied from just behind her.

She whirled around, her gaze reaching only to the middle of Nate's well-built chest. His height unnerved her all the more. She tilted her head up to make eye contact with him.

"Do you have a thermometer?" she queried, patting Gracie gently on the back to reassure herself as much as the baby.

"I think I do," Nate said, and then frowned. "Why? Is Gracie sick?"

Jessica shook her head and tried to smile reassuringly. "She feels a little warm, but I'm sure it's nothing to worry about."

"Should I call the doctor?"

"No," she assured him, keeping her voice calm and level. "Babies often run mild fevers when they are teething. That's probably all it is."

One corner of Nate's mouth tipped up in a half grin and he shook his hand in mock pain. "She's teething, all right. For a little nipper with bare gums, she sure can pack a punch. And I noticed she's been drooling a lot more these past couple of days."

"Sounds normal," Jessica agreed, fighting the stinging lump of emotion growing in her throat. Her own baby, Elizabeth, had only just cut her first two bottom teeth when—

"Here we go," Nate said, fishing a digital thermometer out of the diaper bag. "How do you keep this thing in her mouth?"

Jessica chuckled despite herself. "That would be an interesting trick. I'd like to see you try."

She winked. "Actually, we're going to put it under her arm."

With that, Jessica sat in the chair Nate had abandoned and gently placed the thermometer under the baby's shoulder. Gracie squirmed and verbally protested at being held so snugly, but Jessica held her tight and kept her amused by babbling baby talk at her, repeating whatever random sounds Gracie made.

"I'm glad that's you and not me," Nate said, sitting down next to Jessica and running a palm over Gracie's downy hair. "She's already mad enough at me as it is, for trying to slip her some carrots."

"Fruit is much sweeter and tastier than vegetables," Jessica agreed, smiling at Nate. "As a baby *or* as an adult."

Nate laughed. "Don't let Gracie hear you say that, or I'll never be able to feed her anything more than peaches and bananas."

"It'll get easier," Jessica assured him. "It just takes time and patience."

"And a lot of T-shirts."

Jessica chuckled. Nate had changed one olive-colored T-shirt for another. She wondered if the marine had any other color in his wardrobe.

The thermometer beeped and, unconsciously holding her breath, Jessica peered at the results. Nate leaned forward to look with her.

"Ninety-nine-point-four," Jessica read aloud. "Just remember, when you take a baby's temperature under her arm, you need to add a degree, so that makes it one-hundred-point-four."

"Then she does have a fever," Nate said in alarm, his brow furrowed.

"Only a mild one. She's probably teething, as I mentioned earlier. But you should keep an eye on her, just in case."

"I will," Nate vowed.

"Which, as it happens, brings me to the reason I stopped by in the first place."

Nate arched an eyebrow as Jessica slid Gracie from her arms to his.

"I was under the impression you were going to make use of the day care while you were out job hunting. I started to worry when you never showed."

"Oh, that." Nate shrugged and kissed a wiggling Gracie on the forehead before lowering her into the playpen in the corner of the kitchen, where it was visible not only in the kitchen, but from the living room, as well. "Yes, well, I've had a change of heart."

"How is that?" Jessica was surprised at how her emotions plummeted at Nate's words. She told herself repeatedly that it was none of her business what Nate did with Gracie. While that was probably true, she still cared—maybe too much.

"I decided not to look for a job right away," Nate explained. "I put away most of the money I made when I was in the marines, so I have enough to live off—for now, anyway. I'm not sure if I'm going to be staying around long enough to make it worthwhile for me to pursue anything permanent."

"I see," Jessica said, though she didn't. And she wasn't about to analyze the way her heart dropped at Nate's indication that he wouldn't be around for long.

"Becoming Gracie's guardian is a big adjustment for me. I'm like any parent with an infant, I guess, only I didn't have nine months to prepare for her arrival, so I'm working on a curve."

"I imagine it's a big change for you from being a single man in the military." Jessica paused thoughtfully and then asked the question that was plaguing her. "If you aren't planning to stay at Morningway Lodge, then where will you go?"

Nate snorted. "Anywhere but here."

Jessica wanted to question Nate further about his negative feelings toward the lodge, but she wasn't sure he'd be keen on her poking her nose into his business any more than she already had.

She sighed. "I love it here. It's so quiet and peaceful compared to the ruckus of a big city. You can see and hear God all around you."

Nate stared at Jess, his gaze wide. She spoke so freely about God, as if she was intimately acquainted with Him. It was the way his mother had always spoken of the Almighty, Nate remembered, a feeling of nostalgia washing over him.

But Nate wondered at such naiveté, such sweet and innocent belief as these women shared.

He'd seen the ravages of war firsthand. He knew better than to believe in fairy tales.

He nearly blurted out that he wasn't *looking* for God, but caught himself before he said the words out loud and couldn't take them back.

There was no sense being rude, especially since her faith was clearly very dear to her. He retreated to his usual mode of dealing with issues he didn't really want to address—he clammed up.

Jess didn't appear to notice his sudden silence, and continued thoughtfully.

"Growing up, I lived in Los Angeles. Far too much noise and pollution for me. I'd rather have the clear, beautiful Rocky Mountains any day of the week, thank you very much."

"Is your family still in California?"

She hesitated and her smile faltered, then dropped. Her gaze became distant for a moment, as if she had traveled in her mind to some other time or place; but at length she nodded.

Nate had the impression he'd just intruded where he was not wanted. There was much Jess was not telling him, but he would not presume to pry based on their very short acquaintance. He didn't care for others disrespecting his privacy, and he wasn't going to disrupt her.

He thought the best thing to do would be to change the subject. Baby Gracie's soft babbling had turned to crying, so he reached into the playpen and plucked her into his arms. She quieted at his touch, but her eyelids were heavy and drooping.

"Gracie needs a nap," he commented, bouncing the little girl on his shoulder to soothe her as he crooned. "Don't you, sweetie pie?"

"Looks like," Jess agreed.

"She won't go down unless I rock her," Nate said, nodding his head toward the small living room, where an old wooden rocking chair stood in one corner.

"May I?" Jess asked softly.

"Be my guest." Nate handed Gracie off to Jess, who seated herself in the rocker and began to hum a quiet lullaby.

Even after a week with the baby, Nate still wasn't comfortable when Gracie was fussy. He marveled at how quickly Gracie settled down in Jess's arms. The woman was a natural with children.

He leaned his shoulder on the door frame separating the kitchen from the living area and folded his arms across his chest. There was something just *right* in the way Jess held the baby, he observed; even Gracie instinctively reacted to it.

Nate smiled at the pretty picture Jess and the baby made. Like a little family, almost. Ezra would have been glad to see it, he thought with a mixture of joyfulness and sorrow.

"You'll be a wonderful mother to your own child someday," he murmured.

It was the highest compliment Nate could think to give her, so he was stunned at her reaction.

She turned eight shades of rose before her face bled to a deathly white.

"Are you okay?" he asked when she shot to her feet, swaying precariously. Her grip on Gracie was firm, but he could see that she was shaking.

"I—I'm sorry," she stammered, thrusting the baby at him. "I have to go. Now."

With Gracie wiggling and kicking in his arms, Nate watched helplessly as Jess bolted out the front door and up the path leading away from his cabin. She was running—literally running—away.

He shook his head, bemused. What had he said that had set her off that way? And more to the point, he thought perplexedly, how was he going to fix it?

Jessica's cabin was only a few doors down from Nate's, though it was a steady, uphill climb. She walked—nearly ran—the distance in half the time it usually would have taken her.

By the time she entered the emotional haven of her own small cabin, her chest was heaving and she was gasping for air. Her heart was racing so quickly she could hear it pounding in her ears, but it wasn't only—or even mostly—the physical exertion causing the excruciating pain in her chest.

She was embarrassed and shamed by her actions with Nate, running out on him as she had, without a single word of explanation.

It was just that Nate's off-the-cuff comment had hit her right between the eyes. He couldn't possibly have known what he was saying, and he had most certainly meant his observation as a compliment.

Jessica hadn't been prepared for the maelstrom of emotions that barraged her when she once again held baby Gracie in her arms. The scene had some-how transformed into something pseudo-intimate—*domestic*—between the three of them.

Nate. Jessica. Gracie.

A home and a family had once been the greatest desire of Jessica's heart. But she'd already gone that route, and with devastating results. If she was now alone in the world, it was because she wanted it that way.

As much as she loved being around the baby—or more accurately *because* she loved being around the baby—it would be better for all concerned if she altogether avoided Gracie and her handsome marine guardian.

If she was not careful, her heart would be shattered again, perhaps this time beyond repair.

No, Jessica thought, not even consciously aware she was clenching her fists. She couldn't—*wouldn't*—let it happen again.

Chapter Four

After Nate put Gracie down for a nap, he slung a dish towel over his shoulder and filled the kitchen sink with hot, soapy water.

That was another thing about caring for an infant—the amount of dishes and laundry increased exponentially with the addition of just that one tiny baby girl. He had always had simple needs. This was *way* out of his realm of experience.

Nate set to work scrubbing out baby bottles and bowls of caked-on baby cereal, but his mind was quick to wander back to earlier that afternoon, and the bizarre way Jess had acted.

What was with the woman, anyway?

Nate had noticed her odd behavior from the first time they'd met—the on-again, off-again, hot/cold way Jess acted whenever she was around him. Or perhaps more to the point, when she was around Gracie.

The worst part, though, and the thing, if he was being honest with himself, that stymied Nate the most, wasn't Jessica's unfathomable actions at all. He might not yet understand it, but he could explain it away fairly simply. There must be a reasonable, rational explanation for whatever it was that was bothering her, and eventually, he would figure out what that reason was.

But at the moment, he was dwelling on something else entirely—that flash of time frozen in his mind when the three of them were together in the living room. Jessica's presence had formed it into a homey, domestic atmosphere unlike anything Nate had ever experienced before.

Well, maybe that description was pushing it. His cabin was no more than bachelor's quarters littered with a brand-new smattering of baby items. Not exactly what anyone would describe as *homey*.

But it wasn't so much how the situation had looked. It was how it had felt.

And Nate really liked that feeling.

He realized he was daydreaming and snorted at his own silly behavior.

What was he thinking?

He used the dish towel to scrub his face and force his mind back to the present. His cheeks carried a week's growth of beard on them—because, for the first time in ten years, he could go without shaving.

He shook his head. He'd been alone for far too long to be conjuring up fantasy families in his mind, where none existed in reality.

Still, the idea of a family wasn't completely without merit.

Tamyra, Nate remembered, had rounded out Ezra, taken the rough edges off the heretofore certified bachelor. After the wedding, Ezra had been the happiest Nate had ever seen him. And then baby Gracie had come along and added exponentially to their love. She had, Nate realized, completed the picture.

He recalled being a little envious of his best friend. True love made life worth living, Ezra had told him a dozen times. But Nate'd had his work and his wanderlust, and that had been enough.

At the time.

Now everything was different. Not just in his circumstances, either. His heart felt as altered as the difference between a Colorado blizzard and a California summer. His priorities had shifted from thinking only of himself to having someone else as the center of his existence.

He had a baby to consider now—a little girl who deserved to be raised in a family with both a father and a mother.

Someone like Jess, he realized. A woman who was sweet and caring and who knew how to care for an infant; who would love Gracie the way Nate loved Gracie.

As if on cue, the baby made an enormous pterodactyl scream from the playpen, startling Nate and setting his hair on end. He dashed to the playpen and scooped Gracie into his arms.

Gracie was hot to the touch. He didn't need the thermometer to tell she was burning up with fever. Panic immediately coursed through him, stinging his limbs like an explosion of white-hot nails in an IED.

Snatching the thermometer from the tabletop, Nate rushed to the rocker and took a seat. He attempted to mimic what Jess had done, placing the tip of the thermometer under the baby's arm, but it was a lot more difficult than it looked, even if Gracie wasn't fighting him the way she had with Jess.

She *wasn't* fighting him, but was staring up at him with her big brown eyes as if pleading with him to make her all better.

He didn't know how.

She was frighteningly lethargic.

He checked the thermometer, and another surge of panic coursed through him.

Gracie was running a fever of one hundred and four degrees.

The sound of her cell phone ringing startled Jessica from her sleep. She groaned loudly. She'd nodded off in her easy chair and now her shoulders were stiff and she had a kink in her neck.

Stretching her head from side to side to work loose her muscles, she reached for her purse, which she'd haphazardly tossed on the coffee table earlier. Groggily she dug for the still-pealing phone.

"Hello?" she said, her voice still a little slurred as she wiped the sleep from her eyes with the palms of her hands.

It wasn't surprising that she'd fallen into a deep, dreamless slumber—ever since she was a child, sleep had been her defense mechanism against stress. Her mind and body simply shut down, giving her the rest needed to face her trials afresh.

"Jess?" The one word was laced with so much fear and alarm that Jessica was instantly alert.

"Nate? What's wrong?"

"It's Gracie." Nate's anxious, labored breathing set Jessica right on edge, and she gripped the phone more tightly within her grasp. "She spiked a high fever. I don't know what to do."

"Oh, no!" Jessica inhaled sharply, her whole heart and soul immediately appealing to the Heavenly Father to protect the sweet little baby girl. She tried to quell the rising alarm in her head with little success. "How high?"

"One hundred and four degrees. Jess, what should I do?"

"I'm on my way over," she asserted, trying to keep her voice calm and reassuring despite the way her heart was pounding in her head. Adrenaline coursed sharply through her veins, making her tingly and light-headed.

Whatever promises she had made herself earlier about not seeing Nate or the baby again flew right out the window as if they had never been.

They needed her now.

There was no question that she would be there for them, at whatever cost to her own heart.

She was already reaching for her coat and sliding her feet into her old hiking boots. Her thumb was poised over the phone's exit button when Nate spoke again, his voice rushed.

"I…I phoned you because…because I didn't know who else to call," he stammered.

It occurred to Jessica that the obvious choice would be Vince, who was family. Wouldn't that have made the most sense? Why hadn't Nate called him?

But now was not the time for such questions. She rapidly ticked down the list of vital issues, forcing her mind to concentrate on priority.

"Does she have any other symptoms? A sneeze? A cough?"

"She's pulling on her ear and crying," Nate choked out. "Does that mean anything?"

"Okay, listen, Nate," Jessica said, an instinctive sense of God's strength and peace enveloping her as she took control of the situation. "You need to get her temperature down."

"How do I do that?" he asked, his voice tight. "I just gave her some more medicine, but it will take some time to see any effect. What else can I do?"

Jessica heard Gracie pealing in distress, and her heart turned over.

"Hush, baby girl," Nate crooned. "Uncle Nate's trying to help you, honey. Jess?" he queried uncertainly. "What do I do?"

"Fill the sink with lukewarm water. You need to give her a sponge bath," Jessica directed. "That's going to be the fastest and most effective way to bring down her temperature."

"She's so tiny." Nate's taut voice cracked with emotion.

"And she's not going to be happy about that bath. It's hard to be a parent at times like this."

Jessica realized Nate had referred to himself as Gracie's godfather, but they both knew he was acting in a much greater capacity. "You have to do what is best for Gracie even if it appears to be hurting her."

"I'll do what I have to do," he vowed solemnly, "as long as she gets better."

"She will."

Gracie howled again, her little voice hoarse from screaming.

"I have to go," Nate said.

"Of course. Gracie needs your full attention, which you can't give her while you're still speaking on the phone with me."

"Yeah," he agreed. "But, Jess?"

"Yes?"

"Hurry."

His one word sent a shiver down her spine. "I'm heading out the door right now.

"And, Nate?"

"Hmm?"

"I'm praying for you guys."

She heard the hesitation, and the way Nate quietly cleared his throat. She was on the verge of apologizing when he broke into her thoughts.

"I…" Once again he hesitated. "Well, anyway, thank you. For Gracie, I mean."

"Don't give it another thought," she assured him. "Just get her bathed."

"I'm already on it," he promised.

And she was already out the door.

During the whole ten minutes it took her to rush to Nate's cabin, Jessica petitioned God for Gracie's health and safety. She more than most knew the singular pain of losing an infant. She would never wish that kind of agony on anyone, most especially the kind of man who would put his own life on hold in order to care for a baby who was not his own flesh and blood.

Jessica prayed for Nate as well, that God would give him comfort and peace. Based on what she knew of Nate, she suspected he was not a Christian.

But hadn't God reached Jessica through just such

a tragedy? She prayed it would not take that kind of pain and anguish for Nate to find God.

She briefly considered phoning Vince to let him know what was happening with baby Gracie, but she hesitated, and with good reason. Nate had made a pretty clear statement when he'd called Jessica and not Vince; and from their earlier conversations, it was clear to Jessica that there were definite issues between the two brothers.

Yet tension or no tension, Vince was Nate's brother, his family, and Jessica thought he ought to know what was happening with Gracie. She had been acquainted with Vince a good deal longer than Nate, and she had no doubt that Vince would want to be updated.

But in the end, she decided against calling Vince and simply focused on getting to Nate's cabin as quickly as possible. Whatever the situation was between Nate and his brother, she had to respect his wishes, even if they'd never been spoken aloud.

Even though it was a downhill hike, it felt like forever before she reached Nate's cabin. Several times she thought she should have driven, but she'd been certain she could arrive at the cabin just as quickly on foot. Walking, she could hike straight there. The road was winding and out of the way.

Finally, she broke through the tree line and spied the cabin in front of her. The front door was open, so she let herself in, not wanting to disturb Gracie on the off chance she was sleeping.

She blinked rapidly as her vision slowly adjusted to the darkness of the cabin after having been out in the bright sunshine. Simultaneously, she took in a number of things.

Gracie was sound asleep in her playpen, her chubby legs curled under her. Her arm was wrapped around an enormous, well-worn stuffed orange-and-white-striped fish and her little thumb was tucked in her mouth. Jessica noted with thankfulness that the baby appeared to be resting peacefully, her tiny chest rising and falling in a deep, reassuring rhythm.

Nate was slumped in a wooden chair he'd pulled close to the playpen, his back to the door and his head buried in his hands. Jessica approached him quietly, not wanting to disturb Gracie's slumber.

He jumped, startled, when Jessica laid her hand on his shoulder. She could feel the tension he was carrying in the knotted muscles of his back.

"Hi," Jessica whispered. "I got here as quick as I could. How is she?"

"Jess," Nate groaned as he stood and turned toward her. "Thank you for coming."

A moment later, he swept her into a hug that knocked the wind from her lungs. He clasped her tightly for a few moments. She felt him shudder deeply a moment before he let her go. Concern, compassion and tenderness flooded through her for this man who'd given up so much to take on the care of baby Gracie.

"It's going to be okay," she reassured him when he released her. "*She's* going to be okay. It looks like she is sleeping soundly now, and we can take comfort that God is watching over her."

Jessica wished her words carried more impact, but internally she knew that just because God was in control and, as Jessica had said, was watching over little Gracie, that didn't necessarily mean everything would be all right—at least from her incomplete, staring-into-the-mirror-darkly, human perspective.

God's ways, Jessica had painfully learned, were not always man's ways.

But it didn't hurt to pray.

Nate's face crumpled into dozens of harsh lines, but his gold-flecked eyes held hope. Jessica could see how desperately he wanted to believe her words. His short brown hair was tousled and sticking up every which direction, making him look incongruously and heart-wrenchingly vulnerable next to the muscular strength of the sturdy marine.

"In Isaiah there is a beautiful description of Jesus as the Shepherd over His little lambs," she continued, wanting desperately to comfort Nate. "It goes like this. 'He shall gather the lambs in His arms and carry them in His bosom,'" she quoted softly.

Nate squeezed his eyes shut and Jessica thought the rough-edged marine might be fighting tears.

"I hope so," he said, his voice cracking with emotion. "I really hope so."

Jessica took his hand and led him back to his chair, pushing him gently into his seat before pulling another chair up next to him and seating herself. She reached her arm over the side of the playpen and brushed the backs of her fingers against Gracie's cheek. The baby's skin still felt warm, but not alarmingly so. Jessica was almost certain Gracie's fever was falling.

She sighed in relief. "I think her temperature has gone down some."

Nate swallowed hard and nodded. A muscle twitched in the corner of his strong jaw. "The poor little thing screamed so hard when I gave her a sponge bath that she wore herself completely out. She fell asleep right afterward. I don't mind telling you, she had me scared there for a while."

Jessica struggled for a moment with her own memories, with the sudden way her own baby had been taken from her. Elizabeth had been healthy and happy when Jessica had put her to bed. The next morning she wasn't breathing.

Just like that.

Jessica struggled to contain her emotions, to pull the painful memories back behind the iron wall of her will so Nate would not be able to see what she was feeling on her face.

This was a different situation. It wasn't Elizabeth all over again. Babies got fevers. That was just how it was. And it wasn't necessarily life-threatening. There was no reason for her to panic.

Nate and Gracie needed her strength and support right now, she reminded herself sharply. Breathing deeply, she clenched her hands together and fought for all she was worth.

Nate's groan interrupted her turmoil thoughts, jarring her back to the present.

"I feel so helpless." Elbows on his knees, Nate clasped his hands together and leaned his scruffy chin on them. "I just wish there was more I could *do,*" he admitted roughly.

"There is," Jessica whispered, reaching for Nate's hand. When he glanced up at her, a question in his eyes, she smiled softly. "We can pray."

Nate stared at her for a moment, and then nodded, his jaw tight.

Jessica bowed her head and closed her eyes.

"Heavenly Father, we are thankful that Gracie is in Your tender care. Watch over her and keep her safe. Lord, we ask that You restore Gracie to health and give her little body strength to work through this fever.

"And be with Nate, Lord. Give him wisdom and peace. Amen."

Jessica looked up and caught Nate staring at her, wide-eyed. She wondered if he had prayed along with her, or merely watched her as she prayed. She felt a little self-conscious for a moment, then brushed it off.

What mattered was that she *had* prayed. And God was good. She prayed once again, silently, this time, that Nate would be able to see the grace of God.

Chapter Five

Instead of the peace for which Jess had petitioned, Nate was filled with an inexplicable sense of unease. Still seated in a hard-backed kitchen chair placed next to the playpen, his muscles clenched and ached.

Stifling a groan, he lifted his arms over his head and stretched from side to side, working the knots and kinks out of his shoulders. He wasn't the kind of man to just sit around and wait, and every fiber of his being was itching to move.

He'd been sitting still far too long, watching the even rise and fall of baby Gracie's breath as she slept. She hadn't budged in a couple of hours. Nate didn't know whether that was a good thing or a bad thing, but he took encouragement from the fact that Jess no longer hovered over the baby.

In fact, to his surprise, Gracie wasn't the only one sleeping.

Nate's gaze drifted to the sofa—a two-person love seat, really, as that was all that would fit in the confines of the small cabin—where Jess had curled up and nodded off. Her face had softened during sleep, her arm curled around her neck and a lock of her wavy blond hair lightly brushing her cheek.

His brow furrowed when he noticed her lips turning down, as if she were having a bad dream. In the short time Nate had known her, Jess was nearly always smiling. Her radiant grin was the first thing he'd noticed about her, and it bothered him that somehow she'd lost her peace during sleep.

His fingers tingled with the unfathomable urge to brush that lock of hair off her cheek and smooth the frown from her lips.

Nate had told her it was fine for her to leave, now that the crisis with Gracie appeared to have passed, but Jess wouldn't hear of it. Her chin, which gave the point to her heart-shaped face, had jutted out stubbornly at the mere suggestion.

She was the sweetest, kindest woman he'd ever had the pleasure to know; yet it occurred to him that he might like her to have his back in a fight. Her strength of character, which Nate thought made her faith so vibrant, was remarkable.

And, at the moment, much appreciated.

Secretly, Nate had been glad of her stubborn insistence that she stay, though he'd never admit it out loud. Gracie might be out of immediate danger, but her temperature had spiked very quickly before. He didn't want to go through that kind of a scare again.

Ever.

Not alone, at least. With Jess here, circumstances didn't feel quite so black.

He knew he should be taking the lead from Jess and rest while the baby was sleeping, but try as he might, he couldn't shut off his brain. Usually he exercised his way to exhaustion, but that was impossible given the circumstances.

What he wouldn't give for a nice, long, head-clearing run. It sure would beat sitting here over-thinking everything.

But he wasn't about to leave Gracie's side, not for the hour or more it would take him to get in a good workout. All the same, he found he could no longer sit quietly with his thoughts. Maybe a breath of the fresh, cold mountain air would calm his heart, if not clear his head.

He stood quietly, smiled down at Gracie for a moment, and then tossed a blanket over Jess's shoulders. He let himself out the front door, careful not to let the screen door slam on his way out.

With a sigh, he jammed his hands into the front pockets of his jeans and took a cleansing breath of the crisp air. He stepped into the darkness, away from the soft stream of light streaming from the front window of his cabin. The gravel crunched under the soles of his sneakers.

Why was he so uneasy? For sure, part of it was Gracie's illness, but that wasn't all of what was making his gut clench.

"I love that baby girl," he said aloud, his breath frosting in the air. "I'd do anything for her."

Nate scrubbed his fingers into the short ends of his hair as he stopped under the shadow of a pine and looked up at the stars. He'd forgotten how full the night sky appeared here at the lodge.

Whom, he wondered, did he think he was address-ing with his rambling thoughts?

God?

That smacked of hypocrisy. He'd never been a praying man.

Not until today, anyway.

Not until Jess had taken his hand and spoken to God so simply and expectantly on his and Gracie's behalf. She had voiced petitions Nate couldn't have even begun to put into words.

But he'd been *thinking* about it, hadn't he?

Or maybe more accurately, he'd been feeling it. He might not ever have considered praying aloud, but that hadn't stopped him from hoping there was a God watching down on Gracie in His mercy.

And God had answered. Hadn't He?

In Nate's initial rush of panic over Gracie's high fever, God had sent Jess. Or rather, she'd come when Nate had called her, but from where he was standing, that was the same thing. And now it appeared Gracie was going to be fine.

Maybe she had never been in any real danger, he supposed. Be that as it may—her fever was down, and she looked to be over the worst of it.

Thank God.

But thanking God didn't seem to be enough. Not to Nate. If he was going to acknowledge God, he ought to be *serving* God. It only made sense, and Nate was nothing if not pragmatic.

"I'll do it," he said aloud into the darkness, adding a clipped nod for good measure.

"Do what?" asked a sleepy-voiced Jess, stepping from the shadows.

Startled, Nate's heart hammered in his chest as he turned to the sound of her voice.

"I thought you were sleeping."

Her hair was mussed from napping, which, Nate thought, was somehow endearing. She had wrapped herself in the blanket he'd covered her with earlier, and he could see her breath on the crisp air.

She arched her eyebrow and pursed her lips, acknowledging that she was completely aware he'd just deliberately dodged her question.

With an unexpected wave of amusement, he realized he was out in the cold weather with nothing heavier than a T-shirt and jeans, and was pacing around speaking out loud to himself.

He must look like a real nutcase.

He felt mirth bubbling up in his throat, and for the first time since the night Ezra had died, he felt the tremendous, ominous weight in his chest lighten and dissipate.

He threw back his head and laughed.

When Nate laughed, his entire countenance changed.

The night was dark, with only a sliver of a moon, but Jessica was close enough to see the feathering of laugh lines around his gleaming golden eyes and the indentation of the adorable little dimple that suddenly appeared in his left cheek.

It was the first time Jessica had seen Nate laugh, and her heart turned right over, even as an answering smile drew the sides of her lips upward.

"You should do that more often," she murmured, stepping closer.

"Do what?" he asked, punctuating his question with another chuckle. "Talk to myself?"

"Laugh," she answered, giggling. "It looks good on you."

"Like a crazy man?"

It occurred to her that Nate *was* acting a little out of the ordinary. It wasn't so much that he was talking to himself—she'd been guilty of an occasional soliloquy when she was the only one in the room—but rather the fact that he was outside in a short-sleeved shirt in weather cold enough to frost his breath.

The thought made her shiver, and she pulled the woolen blanket more closely around her shoulders. Warmth immediately washed over her, and it wasn't just from the blanket. She hadn't covered herself with a blanket when she'd dropped off to sleep on the sofa.

She hadn't meant to sleep at all.

Yet she had.

And sometime after that, Nate had thought to pull a blanket around her.

It had been a long time since anyone had done anything to care for her. She prided herself on her newfound independence, but Nate's thoughtfulness warmed her nonetheless.

"Are you cold?" Nate asked solicitously.

"A little," she admitted. "But not nearly as cold as you must be."

He looked down at his bare arms as if just now realizing he was without a coat, and then he threw back his head and laughed again.

Jessica took a step back. Maybe the man *was* off his rocker.

"Not crazy," he assured her as he turned her by the shoulders and pressed her back toward the warmth of the cabin. "Just punchy, I guess. You'd think I'd be used to sleep deprivation after ten years in the marines, but that doesn't hold a candle next to this—caring for an infant 24/7."

A sudden wave of sadness gripped Jessica's heart, but she pushed it away and forced herself to smile up at the gruff marine who was now holding the cabin door open for her.

"No? Go figure."

Nate followed her inside, shaking his head emphatically as he went.

"Not even close. Frankly, I don't know how parents do it."

Jessica leaned over the playpen to check on Gracie. The baby was awake and had rolled onto her back, staring up at Jessica with her enormous brown eyes and sucking steadily on her thumb.

Jessica smiled down at Gracie, reaching for her just as the baby crinkled up her face and started to wail.

"That's easy," she told Nate as she tucked baby Gracie to her shoulder and patted her back. "It's love. Pure and simple."

His smile never leaving his face, Nate stepped forward and kissed Gracie's cheek. His crisp, musky scent followed his movement, and Jessica couldn't help but inhale deeply, her head reeling.

"And who wouldn't lose their heart to little chubby cheeks like these?" he asked softly.

Gracie reached for Nate, and Jessica handed the baby off to him, her heart skipping a beat at the sheer delight radiating from Nate's eyes.

"She feels cool," he said, rubbing his cheek against Gracie's. "I think her fever must have broken."

Jessica placed the backs of her fingers against

Gracie's forehead and then nodded in agreement. "She's definitely doing better. Why don't you check her temperature with the thermometer and I'll see if I can't rustle her up a bottle."

Nate nodded and took a seat in the rocking chair, propping Gracie on his lap.

"The formula is in the cabinet over the sink, and there's bottled water in the fridge."

Nate already had the thermometer under Gracie's arm and the baby was protesting loudly, so Jessica moved to the kitchen, finding all the equipment just where Nate had indicated. She went to work, quickly mixing the formula in a clean bottle she took from the strainer.

She felt oddly at home puttering around in Nate's kitchen, knowing he and Gracie were waiting for her just around the corner. She surprised herself sometimes. At times painfully shy, she usually had to forcefully put herself out there, but with Nate and Gracie, she felt natural.

Comfortable.

And that thought in itself was enough to make Jessica's emotions immediately swing to the polar opposite, until her nerves were stinging with the urge to flee.

She could not afford to get too *comfortable* with Nate.

He was leaving.

Soon.

He'd said as much, earlier that day. He was only here to see his sick father.

And then...

And then *nothing*.

There was absolutely no sense dwelling on the inevitable.

With a sigh, she placed the bottle in the small microwave on the counter and punched the start button, warming the milk for a few seconds.

Nate had called *her* when Gracie became ill. But then again, she was the resident child-care expert. And even if there was something more to it than that, there *couldn't* be more to it than that.

Jessica knew she had to have a care after her own heart. She wasn't ready for any kind of relationship with a man, especially a man with a baby. She wasn't sure she ever would be.

And how foolish was it to even be considering any of this? There was a baby in the next room howling for her bottle.

"That's a good sign," Jessica commented as she entered the living room and handed Nate the bottle. "Her fussing, I mean. It shows she's feeling better."

Nate chuckled as Gracie rooted for the bottle. "If you say so."

Jessica slid onto the sofa, tucking her legs underneath her. "I do. Gracie obviously caught a touch of something, but I think the worst is behind her."

"Thanks to you."

Jessica shook her head. "You know I can't take the credit. The glory belongs to God."

To her surprise, Nate nodded his agreement.

She smiled. "But I'm glad I could be here for you and Gracie."

"Not as glad as I am."

"Which does raise a question," she continued,

knowing she was headed into deep water but unable to stop herself from asking.

"Go ahead," he encouraged when she didn't jump right in with her question. "It's okay."

"If it's none of my business, just tell me it's none of my business."

Nate's jaw tightened almost imperceptibly, but he nodded for her to continue.

"Why didn't you call Vince today?"

The muscles in Nate's neck strained as he swallowed hard and his jaw was equally tight. He didn't immediately answer.

"I've known Vince for almost a year now," she explained. "I think he would have wanted to be there to support you and Gracie."

Nate scowled.

"I know he would," she amended hastily.

"No," he snapped, then shook his head, inhaled and exhaled harshly. "I've had the unfortunate experience of being around Vince a lot longer than you have. Trust me. I know him. He doesn't want anything to do with me. I'd hoped things would change when I came back home, but they didn't."

"But Gracie…"

"I'm not saying Vince has anything against Gracie. It's me he doesn't like. There's a lot of bad blood between the two of us."

Jessica didn't know what to say. She couldn't imagine her employer being painted with the large, harsh strokes Nate was using, but she knew that to Nate at least, that was how Vince appeared.

"I'm sorry," she said, resting her hand on his forearm. "I shouldn't have brought up the subject. I can see it's touchy."

"And I'm sorry I snapped at you," Nate responded, his voice reticent. "You inadvertently touched my hot button and I overreacted."

"I'm sorry," she said again.

"Don't be. My frustration is not with you. I wish there was some way to bridge the gap between my brother and me. For Gracie's sake, if not mine. But honestly, I don't see that happening."

"There must be some way." Jessica didn't have a clue as to what that might be, though, so she clamped her mouth shut.

When would she ever learn to think first and speak later—to mind her own business?

"I'm open to suggestions," he quipped, but he frowned as he said it.

Jessica took the unspoken hint, judging what Nate really meant, and not what he said. "And I am officially butting out and keeping my mouth shut."

They both chuckled, but Jessica felt as if she'd broken the tenuous personal bond which had formed between them, and she wondered how to get it back.

"Too little, too late," she muttered. She hadn't really meant to say the thought aloud, and certainly not loud enough for Nate to overhear her.

"Not at all," he assured her.

She felt her face reddening under his amused gaze, but he winked at her, putting her at ease. His features looked far less strained and his smile was genuine.

If he could let it go, could she do any less?

"Believe me," he continued, "nothing you said is

anything I haven't been thinking about since before I set foot back on Morningway grounds."

"I hope…" Jessica started, and then she stammered to a stop. "I'll pray for you."

"Thank you. I need all the help I can get."

Jessica's eyebrows rose. Nate sounded sincere—genuinely earnest. She prayed she wasn't imagining things, that Nate's heart was actually shifting toward an authentic faith in God.

It sure looked that way.

Trauma had that funny effect on people, and she should know. What was the old saying? There were no atheists in foxholes?

"I'm not blaming everything on Vince," he explained, his voice low and gruff as he tenderly gazed down at the baby in his arms. "I believe you when you say Vince is a good person. Ten years can change a man. I'm living proof of that."

He paused and scrubbed a hand down his face. "The truth is, I burned a lot of bridges when I left Morningway Lodge ten years ago.

"I was young and foolish and headstrong. And I had a chip on my shoulder the size of Colorado. The day I turned eighteen, I took off and joined up with the marines. I didn't tell Vince—or my pop—that I was leaving. I just went. I wrote them a letter from boot camp. I suppose, given those circumstances, I can't blame Vince for holding a grudge."

"Oh," Jessica breathed, then clapped a hand over her mouth.

He paused and looked up, his golden gaze warming hers. His slightly twisted smile was self-deprecating and apologetic.

"So anyway, you can imagine that my pop won't be too happy to see me, either."

"You haven't seen him yet." She hadn't meant to form her thoughts as a statement, but she was belatedly aware it came out sounding that way.

Nate shook his head.

"I might have been wrong about Vince," she said softly. "But I think you should visit your father. He's not feeling well."

Nate shifted Gracie to his shoulder and patted her softly on the back. He stared at Jessica a moment, his brow low over his eyes, and then nodded.

"I know. When I heard about his stroke, I was on my second tour of duty in Iraq, so I couldn't come home to see him. I understand he's gotten worse recently." His voice was laced with regret, and his feelings showed in the way his lips turned down at the corners as he spoke.

"You should go see him," she reiterated, thinking of the last time she'd seen the old man several weeks ago. He hadn't looked well even then. As Nate had said, he had taken a turn for the worse recently and was confined to his room.

"I will. I guess that just goes to show you what a coward I am."

A coward? A man who'd served his country in the war, defusing bombs so his comrades would be safe? A man who had…

"I don't think anyone would call you a coward, Nate," she said softly. "You stepped up and took the guardianship of your best friend's baby. I think that shows great depth of character."

Nate's gold-specked eyes glowed with the compliment. "Thank you. That means a lot, coming from you."

Jessica shuddered inwardly. Nate didn't know what he was saying. She was the biggest coward of all.

"And you're right," he continued. "I do need to see my father. He's the reason I came back to Morningway Lodge in the first place, although I admit I've been a little sidetracked since I've been here. But I will go and see him," he vowed. "And soon."

Chapter Six

Jessica had never been a late sleeper, not even on weekends. And today was no exception.

The past week had flown by, between work and checking on Nate and Gracie every evening. She never stayed long, not wanting to throw the baby off her newly formed routine. Gracie had, Jessica noted, recovered nicely from her fever and was busy trying to learn to crawl around Nate's cabin.

It was Saturday morning, exactly a week after Gracie had spiked her high fever. Jessica was up with the sun, despite having had a deep, dreamless sleep the night before. Though she'd had a full eight hours, she felt as if she'd had no rest at all.

Nate's words to her the week before had echoed through her mind, taunting her incessantly. Though their conversations over the past week hadn't gone beyond remarking about the unusually crisp fall weather and Gracie's happy recuperation, Jessica distinctly felt there was always something unspoken hanging in the air just over their heads.

She had been absolutely sincere when she'd complimented Nate's character. He was the bravest and strongest man she knew.

But it bothered her that her good opinion was obviously so important to him. His warm, golden gaze had said as much as his words, and his words had been shocking enough.

He had somehow erroneously set her on a pedestal, though she couldn't conceive of why.

And he was *wrong*.

So utterly wrong about her.

Sweeping her hair back into a ponytail, she threw on sweatpants and a hoodie and her favorite pair of running shoes and, after stretching, took off jogging down a well-worn path by her cabin.

Her daily morning jog was her quiet time, the time she lifted her burdens to God and found peace and sustenance for the day ahead.

But this morning she found it hard to pray. Her mind was so jumbled she couldn't even put coherent thoughts together, much less lift them to the Lord.

When—and more to the point, *how*—had her life become so complicated?

She had come to Morningway Lodge to retire from the mainstream world, and she had worked hard for the peace and stability she had attained in her life. She held it to her heart and guarded it close.

And then one day a rough-edged marine and his baby girl had arrived at the lodge and had changed everything. That was the *when,* and probably, she thought wryly, the *how,* as well.

She had felt compelled to visit Nate and Gracie every evening after work this week, just to see how the baby was doing, or at least that was what she told herself. Avoiding them wasn't even an option. She had come too far to turn back now.

Truthfully, she didn't even want to try.

Jessica recognized the trust Nate had placed in her by admitting the mistakes he made in his youth. She sensed he wasn't the type of man to give much away, and she felt honored and humbled that he'd chosen to share about his life with her.

She had a lot to learn from Nate—a man who had acknowledged his past and vowed to move forward. Jessica knew herself not to be nearly that strong. She had buried her past rather than acknowledging it.

She winced at the sudden stitch in her side. She'd been running full-force without realizing it. She would have laughed at herself if she could have caught her breath enough to do so. Shaking her head at her own lack of sense, she slowed her pace to a jog and then turned back toward her cabin.

She was hiding the truth. From everyone. She'd buried the past, as much as anyone could who'd been through the type of trauma she'd faced.

Certainly no one at Morningway Lodge knew of her struggles, and that was the way she liked it.

And how she would keep it.

At least for now.

In the meantime, she decided, she would be a friend to Nate. If she was cautious with her heart, there would be no harm done.

She would be careful. Nate had told her he was leaving soon, and all that would be left in his wake would be a few happy memories of the time she had shared with him and Gracie.

* * *

It was a little early to call on Jess, but Nate had decided to move forward with his plan to see his father; and to do that, he needed Jess's help.

Gracie was doing fine. Her fever was long gone, and she was back to happily waking at dawn. In the amazing resilient way of small children, the baby had bounced back to good health. Her color was excellent and she was merrily complaining about the pureed squash Nate tried to feed her. It was almost if the previous week's crisis had never happened.

After his own quick breakfast of toast and strong coffee, he bundled Gracie up in a one-piece pink snowsuit with a furry hood that Nate thought made her look like a little Inuit baby. He chuckled as he strapped her into her baby backpack and set off for Jess's cabin.

When he arrived at her cabin, he knocked quietly at first, and then a little louder. Jess didn't answer the door, and he assumed she was still sleeping. It was Saturday, after all.

He turned to go, thinking he would return later, at a more acceptable hour of the morning.

Just as he stepped away from the door, he spotted Jess approaching at a jog, her short blond ponytail swinging behind her. Her cheeks were pink from the cold and exertion, and she was out of breath.

"Nate," she called, coming to a halt before him and leaning her palms against her knees to catch her breath. "What's up? Is Gracie okay?"

Nate grinned and turned to the side, dipping his shoulder so Jess could see the baby bundled on his back. "She's fine. Her fever is gone and she's back to disliking the vegetables I attempted to feed her this morning. Emphasis on *attempted*."

Jess laughed, her light tone echoing in the crisp air. "Babies are amazing, aren't they? They bounce back from sickness so…"

Her sentence came to an abrupt halt just as her face fell. She pinched her lips together tightly and squeezed her eyes shut, but not before Nate had glimpsed the sheer pain and agony in her gaze.

She was hurting.

She didn't say so out loud, but Nate knew it as sure as he knew the beat of his own heart.

Without a second thought, he wrapped his arms around her and pressed her to his chest. She didn't protest, but curled into him as if seeking shelter in his arms.

Emotion welled in his throat. More than anything, he wanted to protect this woman, to defend her against whatever grief was chasing her, to erase the pain in her gaze.

She had been there for him when he needed her. How could he do any less for her?

"Quickly," Jess finished, her voice muffled in the fabric of his brown leather bomber jacket. "Babies heal so quickly."

Jess took a step backward. Nate took the hint and released her, though he kept his hands on her shoulders as he gazed down at her, trying to read her expression.

Her eyes were bright, but her features were calm. There was hardly a trace of distress left over for Nate to see.

What had just happened?

Jess was smiling up at him, and as far as he could tell, it was genuine. Nate admittedly had little experience where women were concerned. Were they all in possession of such quick-changing moods, or was it only Jess who acted that way?

Clueless. He was absolutely at a loss.

"What just happened?" he asked aloud.

"I'm sure I don't know what you mean," she replied with a dismissive wave of her hand; but she couldn't hold his gaze. Her eyes flickered to a spot just over his left shoulder.

Mind your own business.

She didn't have to say the words aloud for the message to come through loud and clear. Nate felt a little rejected by her emotional retreat, as well as experiencing a sharp sense of discouragement that she didn't trust him enough to confide in him.

He'd poured out his heart to her last week, and yet was receiving nothing in return. He knew he hadn't been wrong to trust her, but he wished with all his heart that she could trust him.

Then again, he reminded himself, the bond of friendship they had formed was unusual—and swift— forged on the heels of crisis.

"Okay," he murmured. He tried to shrug, but the backpack weighed his shoulders down.

"Okay," she agreed, taking another step backward and completely out of Nate's reach. "And why are you here, again?"

"Oh, that," Nate said, bemused for a moment as his mind grappled to catch up with her.

Being with Jess really did a number on him. He

was so turned around he had almost forgotten why he'd come in the first place.

Anticipation pulsed through him, followed quickly by a strong case of nerves. "I've been thinking about what you said."

She raised her brow. "What did I say?"

"About visiting my pop," he concluded eagerly. "Gracie is doing so much better this morning that I thought now would be a good time."

"I agree," she said, smiling her encouragement and making Nate's head spin even more.

"I know the day care isn't open today, but I hoped you could watch Gracie for me."

She nodded. "I could do that. But don't you think your father will want to meet his precious new little granddaughter?"

Nate winced, recalling the cool reception Vince had given him on his homecoming. Nate had no reason to believe Pop would be any more responsive.

Then again, Vince *had* been kind to the baby. Maybe Gracie would help break the ice.

No. He couldn't risk it, and he wouldn't use an innocent baby as a shield.

"I don't know how this is going to go down," he explained, his voice gruff. "I've given Pop a lot of reasons to be angry with me. I don't want Gracie caught in the crossfire of my mistakes. I've noticed how she picks up on everyone's emotions, and I don't want to take the risk of upsetting her."

Jess laid a hand on his forearm. "I appreciate how you put Gracie's needs before your own."

Her warm gaze reinforced her words. Nate squared

his shoulders, feeling a good inch taller just because of her radiant smile.

Jess believed in him.

It was a novelty.

Outside of the marines, where he had naturally excelled and had won the respect of all his men, Nate hadn't much experience in being built up. His own family had done nothing over the years but tear him down.

"I'll tell you what," she continued. "How about I run in and change my clothes, and then Gracie and I can accompany you up to the main lodge."

His heart lit up and he knew it must show on his face. "You'd do that for me?"

"Of course." She waved a hand as if brushing the thought away.

He wondered if she had any idea just what a special woman she was.

He wanted to tell her right there on the spot, but he'd never been particularly good with words, and at the moment, he felt more tongue-tied than ever. In the end, he simply nodded.

"I can stay in the dayroom with Gracie while you are visiting with your father," she said, cementing her new plan. "Then, if everything goes well—and I really think it will—Gracie will be right there in the building, making it much more convenient for you to introduce her to her grandfather."

Nate didn't have Jess's faith that his meeting with Pop would go well, and he laid the blame for that squarely on his own shoulders; but he smiled anyway.

How could he not, when Jess had caught him up in the excitement of the moment?

"Thanks," he choked out.

Jess waved him off again. "It's nothing. I'm glad to help."

It wasn't _nothing_.

It was everything. And so, Nate was beginning to realize, was this woman.

With Nate and Gracie waiting just outside her cabin door, Jessica hurried to change from sweatpants into jeans and to quickly run a brush through her hair, which was rather tangled from having been in a ponytail. As she worked, she prayed fervently.

She would have liked to think her motivation was pure and blameless, and not the self-serving petition she knew it to be.

If Nate reconciled with his father—and she had been speaking from her heart when she told Nate she believed that would happen—then maybe Nate would have a reason to stick around Morningway Lodge a little longer. And even though she knew such an occurrence would put her heart at risk much more so than it already was, she couldn't help but wish it to be so.

The day was cool but clear, so she and Nate decided to walk the short distance to the main lodge. Jessica chattered on about inconsequential things as they went, holding up the entire conversation all on her own. Nate made polite one-word responses and little else.

She was a little self-conscious about being the one doing all the talking, but she sensed Nate's mood shifting inward. Every time a period of silence overtook them—meaning Jessica stopped talking for any length of time—the mood between them felt uncomfortable to her and, she thought, to Nate as well.

While he didn't contribute much to the conversation, he clearly appreciated the distraction.

So she kept talking—about the weather, her work at the day care, descriptions of some of the more colorful guests and their children who'd inhabited the lodge over the past year.

It wasn't until they'd entered the main lodge and Nate was fumbling with his backpack that she stopped talking. She steadied the backpack as Nate slipped it in front of him, and then tucked her hands under Gracie's shoulders while he worked the baby's legs loose from the tight material.

She kissed Gracie's soft cheek before tucking her against her hip and flashed Nate her most encouraging smile. "Well, I guess this is it."

Nate's lips pursed for a moment as he swallowed hard and worked his fingers through the short tips of his brown hair. "Yeah. I guess it is."

"Is what?" came Vince's voice from the front desk. Jess hadn't seen Vince standing there when they'd entered; and if the way Nate's shoulders visibly tightened and the slant of his clenched jaw was any indication, neither had he.

Nate didn't answer, and Jessica took her cue from him, remaining silent as Vince approached. Unconsciously, she tightened her hold on Gracie, then purposefully relaxed again, knowing the baby would respond to the cues she was getting from Jessica.

"How's my little niece?" Vince asked in the high-pitched singsong voice men used with children and animals. He reached for Gracie, and when the baby held out her arms to him, Jessica had no choice but to relinquish the baby to him.

"Oh, you are a sweetheart," Vince crooned as Gracie laid her plump little hands on his face. Vince kissed the baby's forehead, and then turned to Nate.

"How's fatherhood treating you? You ready to wave the white flag in surrender yet?"

Jessica thought Vince's tone was teasing, but she didn't miss the way Nate drew himself up, his shoulders tight and his fists clenched against his sides.

"I don't surrender," he informed Vince through gritted teeth, his gaze narrowing. "Not now, and not ever. Just so we're straight."

Vince shrugged as if he didn't care one way or the other, but his gaze became hooded.

Jessica remembered Nate's comment about the bad blood between the two brothers, but all she could see was two grown men acting as mulish and stubborn as a couple of quarrelsome little boys. Each man was clearly taking his cues from the past, when they'd both been hotheaded teenagers.

Didn't they realize they were both grown men now—capable, at least in theory, of talking through their problems as adults?

Jessica's gaze shifted from Vince's closed expression to Nate's open glower.

Obviously not, Jessica thought, pressing her lips together to keep herself from grinning, knowing any humor she found in the situation would only add kindling to an already sparking blaze.

If she didn't step in and stamp out the fire right now, she thought the two men might regress even further—into an all-out brawl.

Men.

She shook her head and stepped between them, stopping just shy of holding her hands palm out to stop them from advancing on each other.

"How would you like to spend some time with your new little niece, Vince?" she asked in a firm but placating tone.

"Well, sure. I'd love to," he said, then frowned. "If Nate doesn't have a problem with it."

Nate glared at him.

"Why do you ask?" Vince queried, blatantly ignoring Nate as his attention shifted to the baby he still held in his arms.

Nate stepped to Jessica's side. "I'm here to see Pop. Jessica is keeping the baby out here for me while I go in to visit."

Jessica let out a breath she hadn't even realized she'd been holding as the tension, while still fairly high-strung between the two men, dissipated enough that she was fairly certain one wouldn't suddenly lunge at the other.

Fairly certain.

"Are you?" Vince asked, his voice cool.

"Unless you have a problem with it," Nate responded, echoing Vince's earlier sentiments.

Vince's eyebrows arched and he shook his head.

"Not at all. About time, if you ask me. I didn't tell Pop you were back home, like you asked. He'll be surprised to see you."

"That's one way to describe it," Nate answered, his voice so low that while Jessica barely heard the statement, she was sure Vince had not.

Slipping her hand into Nate's, she squeezed reassuringly. "Take your time with your father, Nate. I'll stay here with Vince and Gracie. There's no reason to rush."

Nate met her gaze, his eyes at once apologetic and grateful. He clipped a nod.

"I'll be back soon," he said, and then made a smooth, military about-face and strode toward the hallway.

Jessica watched him go, praying once again that Nate wouldn't find things with his father as bad as he imagined them to be. After what she'd just witnessed between Nate and Vince, she was no longer so sure about Nate's reception with his father.

And if things went poorly, she might be saying goodbye to Nate and Gracie much sooner than she would have thought. Her stomach tightened uncomfortably at the same time her throat closed. If Nate and Gracie left Morningway Lodge, would her heart leave with them?

Chapter Seven

It didn't take Nate more than a minute to reach the suite of rooms located on the far end of the first-floor hallway. He knew right where they were. These had been his parents' rooms when Nate was growing up, with the boys sharing the room across the hallway. Now it was just Pop alone in the suite. Nate wondered if Vince still occupied the room across the way.

Nate hesitated in front of the door, noting how the glass door at the end of the hallway, which gave clients an easier access to their rooms from outside, was shaking from the breeze. He could feel the chill seeping through the edge of the glass door, and made a mental note of it, thinking it ought to be repaired. Not that it would be easy to mention a suggestion with any negative connotation attached to it to Vince.

Not that Vince would care to listen to any of *his* suggestions. Nate knew he had lost any claim to Morningway Lodge when he'd entered the military. That was how he wanted it to be, and it was a sure bet Vince didn't want him interfering in any way.

Shaking his head to dislodge the unwelcome

thoughts, Nate rapped three times on the door to his father's room. He waited a moment, and then when no one answered, he tried the knob.

It turned. Thinking his father might be resting, he swung the door open on silent hinges and let himself into the room.

The living quarters were much the same as Nate remembered them. Several of his mother's cross-stitched pictures still hung on the walls, and the furniture was the same—two plump old blue fabric easy chairs sat at an angle from an equally worn cream-colored sofa and a knotted pine coffee table that lent the décor a quaint look Nate had always loved. A small dining table and two hard-backed chairs stood in the far corner.

No need for a kitchen, Nate knew, for the chef in the main lodge always brought in meals for them. An open doorway in the middle of the right wall led to the tiny bed and bath.

It was only after he'd taken a moment to draw in his surroundings that Nate noticed his father, tucked into a wheelchair and facing the window. The curtains were open and the sun was streaming down on the old man, giving Nate the peculiar feeling he was looking at someone larger than life.

And that, Nate acknowledged silently, was what his father had always been to him.

Larger than life.

"I told you I wasn't hungry," Jason Morningway bit out without turning to see who was in the doorway. "Just take it away."

"Pop?" Nate asked hesitantly.

His father jerked, then froze.

"Pop? It's Nate."

"Nate," the old man repeated, wonder in his voice. "My son."

Nate's throat welled with emotion and he tried to swallow it back, but the stinging pressure at his Adam's apple simply wouldn't go away, making it difficult for him to breathe.

Slowly, the old man appeared to regain at least a semblance of use in his upper body, and using his right hand, he put pressure on the switch that turned his chair around. After a moment of adjusting the switch, Jason gazed up at his son.

Nate felt as if he'd been sucker punched in the gut. His breath swept audibly from his lungs.

This was the man who had so completely intimidated Nate as a boy?

Gone was the height and strength Nate remembered. In its place was a tiny, shriveled man confined to a wheelchair, with a flannel blanket tucked around his legs. His gray eyes were filmy and the muscles on the left side of his face drooped slightly.

Nate hadn't realized until that moment how devastating his father's stroke had been. Pop looked eighty, not the sixty-eight years old Nate knew him to be.

"Come here," Jason commanded, and Nate immediately obeyed, for it was the imposing voice that Nate remembered from his youth.

His father stared up at him for a long moment without speaking. Nate noticed the way the old man's shoulders were quivering and thought it might be from strain, so he swiped a hard-backed chair from the dining table and seated himself in front of his father.

He wanted to reach out and touch the old man, if

nothing else to reassure himself that the moment was real, but he didn't move a muscle.

His father had never been the touchy type. Nate could count on one hand the number of times Jason Morningway had embraced him as a child.

So he was surprised when his father lifted his frail right arm and clasped Nate on the shoulder. Nate could feel the chill of Jason's hands through his shirt and he shivered unconsciously.

"Nate," the old man said again. "My son."

"I'm here, Pop," Nate said. "I'm here."

Though he knew it wasn't his fault that he couldn't be here when his father collapsed, that he had been a continent away fighting for his country, he still felt guilty for his absence.

"A marine," Pop said, as if somehow reading Nate's thoughts.

Where Nate had expected anger, he heard pride, and his mind clouded with unexpected sensations.

"Yes, sir. Ten years, now."

The old man wet his dry, split lips with the tip of his tongue and cracked a wavering half smile. "Your mother would have been proud."

Nate's eyes stung with unshed tears. He hadn't cried since he was a small boy, and he wasn't about to do so now, but the pressure behind his eyelids didn't go away even after he blinked repeatedly.

"You've come home," Pop said, as if he'd only now realized the fact. "Why?"

"Yes, well, I don't know, really. And I doubt if I'll be staying."

His father's face fell, and Nate scrambled to bring

the tenuous smile back to Pop's lips. Two minutes with his father and he'd already blown it.

"I have a baby," Nate blurted.

At this awkward pronouncement, Pop's gaze narrowed into an expression Nate was more familiar with. This was the father Nate had expected. Perhaps things hadn't changed as much as they had first appeared.

"You got married?" the old man barked. "Vince never said."

"No, sir," Nate answered. He would have continued his explanation, but Pop cut him off.

"I raised you better than that."

So the man still had some fight in him, did he? Somehow, his father's reaction relieved Nate—Pop the way he had been and not as he was now.

"Yes, sir. I know you did. The baby is not my biological child. She was my best friend Ezra's daughter. My battle buddy in Iraq. When he died, I became Gracie's legal guardian."

"Gracie," his father repeated, testing the name on his lips. "Where is she?"

"A close friend of mine is watching her in the dayroom."

"Well, I want to meet my little granddaughter," Pop said, fidgeting with the blanket on his lap. Nate could see the old man only had one good arm to work with. His left arm lay virtually useless by his side. "How about you bring her to me?"

Nate stretched forward to tuck the blanket around his father and felt a shiver rock through the man.

"Are you cold?" Nate asked solicitously. Central heating kept the lodge at a comfortable seventy degrees, but Pop's skin felt cold to the touch.

"I'm always cold," Pop grumbled. "I can't seem to warm up, not even under a dozen blankets. That stroke of mine nearly did me in. Still might," he said with a disgusted grunt.

Nate wanted to cringe at his father's fatalistic statement. He'd told himself over and over throughout the years he'd been gone that he didn't really care about his family, for they never really cared about him.

But that wasn't true. This was his *father*. Nate loved him despite his flaws.

Nate tucked the flannel blanket more tightly around his father's frail shoulders.

"I'll go get Gracie," he said, deciding the best thing to do was get Pop's mind off his ailments. "It'll just be a moment."

Pop grunted again and turned his chair back toward the window. "I'll be here. Got no place else to go."

The defeatist tone to his father's voice saddened Nate. It was as if the man had just given up. He could understand the feeling, even if he didn't agree with it. Pop was confined to a small set of rooms and a wheelchair.

That would take the fight out of most men, Nate thought.

But not his pop.

Pop was a scrapper and always had been. He'd started a business with little more than a wish and a prayer, and had built it up for himself with his own two hands. He'd worked hard over the years to provide for his family.

Only to have it end like this?

Nate vowed to himself it would not be so.

* * *

Jessica looked up just as Nate entered the dayroom. She tried to read his expression as his gaze met hers, wondering how it had gone with his father, but it was hard to tell.

His eyes were wide and his lips pinched. He looked lost, Jessica thought, like a little boy who'd wandered away from his parents in a department store and had looked up only to find the faces of strangers swarming in and out around him.

She was thankful she was the only one there to witness it. Vince had spent a couple of minutes playing with Gracie, and then had excused himself to go back to the office.

"How did it go?" she asked softly.

Nate didn't immediately answer. Instead, with the gold flecks in his eyes shimmering brightly, he reached for Gracie, who flapped her arms and babbled excitedly at his attention.

"Okay, baby girl," he murmured, swinging Gracie in the air and then kissing her chubby cheek. "Your grandfather wants to meet you."

"Oh!" Jessica exclaimed, releasing the breath she'd been holding. "It went well, then?"

Nate's gaze met hers over the top of the baby's head, and he gave a clipped nod. He smiled, but it didn't quite reach his eyes.

Impulsively, she stood and moved to Nate's side, giving him a quick, spontaneous hug.

"Poor Pop," Nate said, shaking his head. "I had no idea the stroke had debilitated him to such a colossal extent."

"You couldn't have known."

Nate snorted. "Maybe deep down I knew, and I just didn't want to face reality."

"You're here now," she gently pointed out, absently stroking his shoulder.

"Well, I'm too little, too late," he snapped derisively.

"Not at all. How can you say that? He was glad to see you, wasn't he?"

Nate's lips twisted as he nodded.

"And if that wasn't enough, I'm sure baby Gracie is going to make his day."

Nate gazed down at Gracie, and then offered his hand to Jessica. "He seemed anxious to meet her."

"Then what are we waiting for?" Jessica asked, pulling him toward the hallway.

Nate didn't say anything, but he allowed her to lead him down the hallway and back to his father's suite of rooms.

"Pop?" he called, entering the room without knocking on the door this time. "I've brought Gracie."

Jessica had seen Jason Morningway off and on at the lodge, though he had been too ill in the past few weeks to make the foray out to the dayroom to interact with others. He looked a bit weaker than she remembered, but the joy shining from his gray eyes was unmistakable.

"My granddaughter," he announced, wheeling his chair forward. "Thank the Good Lord. I didn't think I would live to see the day."

Nate's hand clenched tightly over Jessica's for a moment, and she gave him a reassuring squeeze back before letting go.

Nate crouched before his father and propped Gracie

up on his knee, so the old man could see her and interact with her.

"Little darling," Jason crooned, reaching his hand toward Gracie.

The baby wasn't shy with strangers; or maybe, Jessica thought, Gracie instinctively knew that Jason Morningway was family. Gracie clasped her little fist over her grandfather's index finger and babbled happily at him.

"She's quite a talker," Jason said with a gruff laugh. "How old is she?"

"Six and a half months," Nate answered with a tentative smile. "And she's already more than a handful, let me tell you."

"As were you," his father countered, a faraway look reaching his eyes. "Even before you were born, you were always on the move. I remember your mother saying she thought you were going to be a circus acrobat. And then as a toddler, we couldn't keep you still for more than a minute. You'd climb on bookshelves, throw your ball through a window. One time you hid in the middle of an apparel rack at a department store and your mother couldn't find you. You scared the wits out of her that day."

Nate flashed Jessica a wide, surprised gaze. Did Jason remember that Gracie was not Nate's biological child? He spoke as if the fact had slipped his mind.

Jessica shook her head briefly. There was no sense pressing the issue with Jason, who would probably forget again the moment they left the room. Strokes could play havoc on the mind.

Besides, Jessica thought, in all the ways that mattered, Nate *was* Gracie's father. There was far more than genetics involved here.

Jason seemed to notice the silent exchange between Nate and Jessica, for his gaze focused on Jessica and the side of his mouth that worked correctly crooked up into a half smile.

"And who is this lovely creature?"

Nate rocked back on his heels, pressing Gracie close to his chest. "I'm sorry, Pop. I thought you already knew her. This is my…" he hesitated "…friend. Jessica Sabin."

Jessica noticed his hesitation and wondered if he'd been about to say something different, but she didn't have time to dwell on it.

"I'm the day care director, Mr. Morningway. I've been here at the lodge for about a year now. We've met before, at a couple of social events."

Jason frowned, the right side of his face crinkling to match the left. "I'm sorry. I don't remember."

"Think nothing of it," Jessica gently assured him. "There are so many people coming and going in and out of Morningway Lodge at any given time, you would be hard-pressed to remember names and faces. After a while, it all becomes a big blur. I can't remember names to save my life—except, of course, for the kids I work with." She chuckled.

Jason settled back in his wheelchair, looking at ease once more. As Nate stood, he flashed Jessica a grateful smile and reached for her hand.

"Jess has been a godsend," he remarked. "She has really helped me out with Gracie. I would have been lost without her. She's the resident expert where babies are concerned."

Jessica shrugged off the compliment, uncomfortable with the way both Nate and his father were beaming at her, as if she were someone special.

Jason's gaze dropped to where Nate's and Jessica's hands were joined, and he smiled crookedly again. "Such a lovely little family you have there, son."

Jason's innocent comment sent such an intense bolt of shock through Jessica that she quivered as if she'd just been struck by lightning. She immediately snatched her hand away from Nate's, feeling almost singed by the contact of his fingers.

She expected the surprise in Nate's gaze as his eyes met hers, but not the golden glimmer that spoke of something else entirely.

Feeling branded by a look that surpassed even the touch of his hand, she quickly turned away, only to meet another familiar pair of eyes as she spotted Vince in the doorway behind them.

Vince was leaning against the doorjamb, his arms crossed in front of him. For the briefest moment, Jessica glimpsed such a look of pain and betrayal that she winced inwardly.

Then, just as quickly, Vince's gaze became hooded under lowered brows. Cold, hard anger jetted from his eyes, replacing any other emotions Jessica had seen just a moment before; so swiftly, in fact, that she wondered if she'd seen anything else at all.

"Right, Pop," Vince growled. "What we have here is the perfect little family. Isn't that just so sweet to see? How incredibly happy you must be that your prodigal son has returned."

Still glowering, Vince turned on his heels and

swiftly stalked away before anyone could offer a reply to his harsh words.

Jessica whirled around, wondering how to diffuse the situation. Not surprisingly, Nate was glowering at the now-empty doorway, and Jason's expression was a mask of confusion, followed by a mixture of acknowledgment and regret.

"Your brother is not happy." Though Jason was stating the obvious, both Nate and Jessica stared at him as if he'd just made some spectacular revelation.

"No kidding," Nate groaned. "I'm sorry, Pop. I never should have come back here. I'm just making things worse for everybody."

"No." Jason's one-word response was clear and shrill and brooked no argument. The foggy look that usually clouded his eyes had dissipated completely and he was looking at Nate with cool lucidity.

Nate's eyebrows rose and his jaw dropped. Jessica thought her expression might mirror Nate's, and she pinched her lips together to make sure her mouth was still firmly closed.

"This is your home," Jason continued. "You belong here. Gracie belongs here."

Privately, Jessica agreed with Jason's assessment, but she knew it would take much more than a few simple words to convince Nate.

"But Vince—" Nate started to argue, and then was cut off by his father's harsh look.

"Vince has not been happy for a very long time. Far before you came back home. I know you think you're the cause of all his troubles, but you aren't. Vince has many things to work through, but it will go better for him if he has his brother's support."

"I don't know, Pop."

Jason jerked his head to one side. "I raised two very stubborn sons."

Jessica pinched her lips again, this time to keep from smiling. She definitely agreed with Jason's opinion of the relationship between Nate and Vince. She had never met two more willful men.

Nate frowned and shrugged, but didn't offer any further comment.

Jason smiled, looking as if he'd won a battle. "Good, then," he said, as if punctuating the conversation. "Now let me see my little granddaughter."

Chapter Eight

It wasn't any real surprise to Nate that Jess had bowed out as soon as they'd left the main lodge. He didn't know whether to be distressed or relieved. Clearly she didn't want to talk about what had happened between Nate and his father—and most especially Vince—and Nate couldn't say that he blamed her.

He bundled Gracie back up in her snowsuit and plopped her into the backpack before swinging it on his back and adjusting the shoulder straps.

"Ready to go, little lady?" he asked the squirming baby.

Gracie patted him on the head, which he took as her version of "Let's go!"

Nate realized he had inadvertently thrust Jess right into the middle of a family squabble. In all fairness, she *had* known Vince longer than she'd known Nate. Not to mention the fact that Vince was Jess's employer. It wouldn't be right of Nate to make her choose between the two of them.

He was certain she'd had no idea what she was getting into when she'd offered her support to him today. *He* hadn't known it would go down like this.

His father, at times lucid and at others frighteningly befuddled.

Vince barging in on their reunion and disrupting what would otherwise have been a tender moment.

Pop commenting on what a sweet little family Nate and Jess and Gracie made. Right out of left field, but dead on the money, Nate thought.

At least on his and Gracie's side of things, it certainly was. The more time he spent with Jess, the more time he wanted to spend with her. Although if he were honest, the look of utter shock and surprise on Jess's face when Pop had made his pronouncement about their *little family* led Nate to believe Jess hadn't thought about it as much as he had—if at all.

Was she just being friendly to a hopeless-case marine and his baby? If the current he felt running so strongly between ran no deeper than that on her side, how was he going to turn the stakes in his favor?

It was more frightening to Nate to face rejection from Jess than to face danger or pain.

The question now was definitely *how,* not *if.* Jess had become too much an ingrained part of his and Gracie's life for Nate to even consider not pursuing a relationship with her. He'd never experienced the kinds of heartfelt sensations he did when he was around Jess. That had to count for something.

He stepped out of the lodge and absently noted that the weather was now cloudy and overcast, kind of like his mood right now, he thought. But he suddenly had to thrust those thoughts aside as he was confronted with a more immediate problem.

Rather than hide out in his office as Nate would have expected his brother to do, Vince was at the side of the lodge, measuring and cutting long sections of two-by-fours, a baseball cap turned backward on his head and a pencil tucked behind his ear.

Nate's first thought was to turn another direction, but it was already too late for that. There was no avoiding Vince now.

Vince, obviously spying Nate, had pulled himself to his full height and allowed the tape measure he was using to snap shut, echoing in the air. He stared at Nate as if he thought him from another planet.

With a sigh, and an immediate, involuntary tightening of his shoulder muscles, Nate trod up to Vince and slid to a stop in the gravel. Vince glared at him, and Nate scowled back.

"What is your problem, man?" he demanded, tightening his hold on the straps of the backpack cutting fiercely into his shoulders.

As soon as the words were out of his mouth, Nate wished them back, but the damage was already done. Vince's brow dropped so low Nate could barely see his blue eyes sparking with anger, and Vince clenched and unclenched his fists as if he was internally fighting the urge to strike out.

Bring it on, Nate thought. This was a long time in coming.

As an angry haze swept over him, he forced himself to take a mental step backward. This wasn't the way to solve their problems.

He was annoyed that his father's reception had been so much warmer than Vince's, but now he'd made it twenty times worse for himself with his big mouth.

His father had been right to call him stubborn. He was that, and a dozen other bad qualities, all wrapped up in a big, oafish military frame.

Would he ever take a clue from Jess and learn to control himself?

"Sorry," he apologized hastily. "I didn't mean that the way it sounded."

Vince's scowl darkened even further. "I know exactly what you meant. Don't try to sidestep the issue and take it back now."

"Look, I said I was sorry," Nate said again, holding his hands out in a conciliatory manner. "What can I do to make it up to you?"

"Ha!" Vince snorted. "What do you think? You're about ten years too late asking that question, little brother."

What, Nate wondered, was *that* statement supposed to mean?

Ten years ago, Vince hadn't wanted anything to do with him. He was nothing more than a roadblock to Vince's ambitions. Because Nate had left, and with his father's subsequent stroke, Vince got everything he wanted—total control of the lodge.

So what was his problem? If that was, in fact, what he had really wanted.

Nate took a long look at his brother—really looked at him—for the first time since he'd returned home. Though he was only thirty years old, his face was weathered and stress lines were already forming. A lock of hair that fell down over his forehead from underneath the baseball cap was a premature silver.

Was this what Vince wanted? Or had all this been thrust on him because Nate had left?

For the first time, he saw his actions through his brother's point of view, and he couldn't help but wonder just how much of Vince's stress and worry *he* had caused when he'd run off to join the military.

"I wasn't thinking of anyone but myself," he said aloud.

Vince quickly masked his surprise, but not before Nate had glimpsed it.

"I apologize, bro. I never realized until this moment how I completely left you in the lurch when I enlisted," Nate continued, suddenly yearning to put all his cards on the table. "Because of me, you've had the burden of running the lodge single-handedly. Maybe that's how you wanted it. Maybe not. But I sure shouldn't have left without telling you I was going."

There was a tense moment while Vince stared at him, slowly ingesting what he'd just said. The mountain, usually rife with sound—the wind rustling through the trees, the river in the distance rushing over jagged rocks, the birds and wildlife—was suddenly painfully silent.

Nate held his breath and waited.

Finally, Vince shrugged.

"What's done is done," he said, sounding lofty and philosophical in his tone. "There's no sense talking about it."

Nate swallowed hard, wondering if this might be Vince's awkward way of showing forgiveness, if it might be the first step in reconciliation between them.

Nate didn't know, but he could hope. The tension didn't leave his shoulders as he held out his hand to shake Vince's.

"I'm glad to be back home," he said huskily. To his own surprise, he realized he meant it.

Vince eyed Nate's extended hand for a moment, then raised one eyebrow and spun away, snapping his tape measure against a beam of wood and concentrating on his project as if he and Nate had never spoken at all.

As if Nate wasn't still standing there, waiting for... *something*.

Nate dropped his arm, experiencing a wave of defeat that nearly overwhelmed him. His father's happy reception had given him a false sense of hope. He should have known Vince wouldn't back down so easily.

If there was a way to get back into Vince's good graces, Nate didn't know what it was.

Back in Vince's good graces?

Ha! Who was he trying to kid?

He'd never been on Vince's good side, and at the rate he was going now, he never would be.

Maybe it was time to buck up and face the truth. He wasn't wanted here. Like he'd said to his father, coming home had done more harm than good.

But, knowing Jess was here at Morningway Lodge, a place that represented all that was bad about Nate's life, could he still consider leaving?

He snorted aloud shook his head.

Not a chance.

His feelings for Jess were simply too strong to ignore, and his brother was just going to have to learn to deal with it, or simply ignore him the way he had done when they were kids.

Because he wasn't leaving.

* * *

Jessica hadn't bothered fussing with a big dinner for herself. Instead, she'd put a can of tomato soup on the stove and grilled a cheese sandwich, washing it down with a tall glass of milk. Usually she enjoyed cooking, even if it was just for herself, but tonight her heart hadn't been in it.

Knowing she was going to be an emotional basket case if she held it all in, she allowed herself the luxury of grieving for the past. There were times, she knew, when the best way around an obstacle was through it, and this had been one of those nights.

She'd taken out her baby album and spent the evening with the paradoxically joyful and heartbreaking memories of her daughter, Elizabeth.

No matter what, she promised herself she would not dwell on the events of the past afternoon; but try as she might, Jason's confused words echoed over and over again in her consciousness.

Such a lovely little family.

She wondered what Nate would have said about his father's observation if Vince hadn't shown up when he did, and then decided it didn't matter.

Okay, so maybe it *did* matter, but she wasn't going to think about it.

When she finally drifted off to sleep late in the evening, it wasn't into her usual stress-induced black void. Rather, her dreams were filled with a handsome marine and his baby girl.

When Jessica awoke the next morning, it was with a joyful heart and a thankful spirit. It was Sunday, and as was her usual habit, she would go to church and worship God, laying all of her burdens down at His feet.

As she suspected, the worship service was just what she'd needed. She returned home with her heart much lighter and her soul refreshed, scrubbed clean and ready for a new week, her focus on God.

Her mind was still humming a praise song as she approached her cabin and exited her SUV, so she did not, at first, notice the note taped to her front door.

When she did, she reached for the ragged piece of paper and tore it off in surprise.

Her name was written in a big, bold script on the back side of an old gas receipt.

Jess—
Gracie and I stopped by your cabin, but you weren't home. Guessing you're at church. Anyway, call me or come by when you have a chance.
—Nate

Jessica crumpled the note in her fist and held it close to her heart, trying to steady the sudden upswing in her breathing pattern. There was simply no denying the way her pulse leaped at the knowledge that Nate wanted to see her, nor the way her gut tightened painfully in response.

It was an oddly pleasant form of torture, she mused thoughtfully; and the funny part was, she was doing this to herself.

What did Nate want?

Could it be possible that he was going to tell her he was planning to stay at the lodge? Permanently?

She smiled to herself as she remembered the

utter joy and relief apparent on his face after he had reconciled with his father.

Did she dare to hope?

But the past clouded her future. In her mind, she acknowledged that having had one bad relationship with a terrible outcome didn't necessarily doom her to an entire lifetime of bad relationships; but in her heart, not so much.

The truth was, she accepted silently, she was a total coward.

She was afraid to fall in love again. Because if she opened herself to loving, she would also open herself to losing.

Was that a risk she was willing to take?

Nate had just put Gracie down for the night when Jess knocked on his door. He grinned broadly as he let her in, especially when he saw the plate of delicious, still-warm-from-the-oven chocolate brownies she'd brought along with her.

He was so excited about sharing the new plan he'd worked up that he would have welcomed a phone call, but it was much better to see Jess's beautiful face in person.

"I got your note," she whispered as she entered the cabin and handed Nate the plate of brownies. "Is Gracie asleep?"

"Yes," he answered in a low voice. "As a matter of fact, I just put her down for the night."

"I'm sorry I didn't make it over before she fell asleep. Is she sleeping well for you?"

Nate smiled. "All the way through the night, most nights."

Jess returned his smile. "See? I told you it would get easier."

Nate laughed softly. "Well, I don't know about that, but the two of us are finally starting to get into a routine together, I think."

Jess peered down into the playpen where Gracie was sleeping, tilting her head to one side as she hesitated, her smile faltering. "You know, I could come back tomorrow. I'd hate it if we accidentally disturbed the baby with our chatter."

"Oh, no, you don't," he said hastily, shifting from one foot to the other. "You're not getting away from me that easily."

Her eyes widened, but he didn't coax the smile from her he had hoped to, with his teasing words, and it made him curious.

The woman acted as if a man had never flirted with her before, and he didn't believe that for a second. He wondered, not for the first time, how such a beautiful, kind woman had ended up holed away in a mountain retreat, all by herself. Why hadn't some lucky man before now swept her off her feet?

Well, he thought wryly, their loss was definitely his gain.

And Gracie's.

If ever there was a woman meant to be a mother, it was Jessica Sabin. He was more appreciative than she would ever know for all the help she'd given him over the past few weeks.

"If you don't mind, we could go sit out on the front porch," he suggested, smiling down at the sleeping baby. He was so excited about his new idea that he wasn't sure he'd be able to keep his enthusiasm in check if they spoke indoors.

"That sounds lovely," she answered. "It's a really nice evening out, compared to how frosty the weather has been lately. Today it almost feels like an Indian summer night."

Nate slipped into his bomber jacket and then held the screen door for Jess and waited until she'd seated herself on the porch step before sitting down beside her. He left the door open so he could hear if Gracie stirred, but he thought they would be able to talk without bothering the baby.

"So, what's up?" she asked after they'd sat a moment in silence. "You've made some decisions?"

He nodded. "In a way, yes. I've been thinking a lot about my future. And Gracie's."

She tensed up, which looked to Nate like a shiver. She was right about the night being mild, but she'd only worn a light windbreaker for a jacket. Even in the summertime, the Rocky Mountains could get cold once the sun went down—and this was not summertime.

He put his arm around her shoulders, thinking to keep her warm, and smiled to himself when she shifted, cuddling in under his arm.

"What have you decided?" She didn't look at him when she spoke, but rather at the shadows of the trees lengthening in the setting sun.

"Nothing permanent, yet." He followed her gaze, for once enjoying the mountain view. Funny how his perspective changed when Jess was around.

"Oh." She sounded a little bit taken aback, and Nate wondered why.

What was she thinking? He wished he knew, but he

didn't know how to form the question to ask her about it, so he mentally dropped the subject and continued with his previous train of thought.

"Anyway," he continued, "I've been thinking about my dad."

"I thought you might be," she commented, and then sighed. "I'm glad that situation worked out for you as well as it did."

"Me, too," he agreed fervently. "I didn't realize that was going to be such a giant step for me. You have no idea how much it meant to me to be reconciled with Pop."

"Oh, I think I might," she disagreed, smiling softly and shyly.

He arched one eyebrow, questioning her without speaking.

She shrugged. "I could see it on your face when you came back from talking to him."

"That obvious, huh?"

"Oh, yes," she said with a laugh. "At least, to me, it was. But then I've always had a gift for being able to discern what someone is feeling, even when they don't say anything out loud."

He squeezed her shoulder. "I believe that. You always seem to know what Gracie needs."

"Babies are easy."

"Ha!" Nate burst out with a spontaneous laugh. "Says you."

She stared at him a moment, her lips pursed. "You're very good with her, you know."

"Do you think?"

"I know. I don't think you give yourself enough credit."

"Hmm."

"I also know, based on the expression on your face, not to mention the note you left taped to my door, that you are dying to tell me something. So just go ahead and spit it out, already."

"Once again, you've read my mind," he teased. He couldn't wipe the grin from his face if he tried. "I do have something I want to get your opinion on. It's about my pop."

Chapter Nine

"I'm always happy to offer my opinion," Jessica answered in the same teasing tone. "So what's going on with your father?"

"Well, when I went to visit him, I noticed that he seemed to be cold. The central heating was working just fine, but he was shivering, even though he had a wool blanket covering him. When I asked him about it, he told me he feels like he can never get warm."

"That's too bad. He has already suffered through so much with that stroke."

"I know," Nate agreed. "I can't get him out of my mind. I want to do something to help him—to make up for the way I wounded him when I left the lodge and joined the marines."

"You don't have to do penance," Jess said softly. "What's done is done. And your father already forgave you, you know."

"Yeah," Nate said on an exhale. "I know. But I still want to do something for him."

"What did you have in mind?"

"I want to build him a fireplace. You know,

something easy on the eye, made out of stone, maybe, that will help him keep warm. I was thinking he could stoke it up as much as he needs to and have a lot more control over how warm he keeps the room."

Jess bounded to her feet, spun around and took Nate's hands in hers. "That's a wonderful idea!" she exclaimed, obviously sharing his enthusiasm.

And his vision.

He stood and hugged her, enjoying the way his heart soared at her encouragement. He was so grateful for her support.

He thought about what it would be like to have her at his side every day for the rest of his life, and he liked the mental picture he drew. How high could he reach with her love?

"You'll have to run your idea by Vince, you know. I don't see how you can get around it."

Her words popped the bubble of Nate's daydream like a stick pin.

Telling Jess had been the easy part.

He'd already known he'd have to get Vince's permission to proceed with his plan. Vince had the final say on every aspect of Morningway Lodge, and what Nate was proposing was a pretty major renovation.

He dropped his arms from Jess's waist and shrugged, hoping he'd pulled off nonchalance but knowing Jess saw right through his bravado.

"Do you think he'll go for it?"

To his relief, Jess nodded. "I think he may surprise you."

Nate snorted. "Highly unlikely. But as you said, I have to speak to him first."

"What are you going to do with Gracie while you work on the project?"

He chuckled and flashed her a goofy grin. "That's where you come in, honey."

She laughed in delight. "I'll admit I was hoping you'd say that."

"I was thinking I'd drop Gracie by the day care on weekdays while I work."

"We'd be happy to have her," she said, her tone suddenly businesslike and efficient.

"There's still an opening, then?"

Jess looked away from him, then chuckled. "For Gracie, I'd *make* an opening. But in answer to your question, yes, we have an opening available."

She had a strange look on her face when she spoke, and she still wasn't looking him in the eye. Nate knew she wasn't telling the whole story.

"What?" he queried playfully. "What are you not telling me?"

Jess glanced away for a moment, her face reddening under his scrutiny.

"I saved it for you," she mumbled under her breath, shrugging as if what she said didn't matter.

"You what?" Nate asked, though he was fairly certain he'd heard her correctly the first time. Still, he wanted to hear her say it again.

"Oh, all right. I'll 'fess up. You know how I feel about—" she paused as if searching for words, and if it were possible, her face flushed with even more color "—about Gracie."

Nate cocked an eyebrow, feeling certain that

wasn't what she'd been about to say. She had mentally amended her statement from…?

A slow grin spread over Nate's face as he inwardly answered his own question. "Go on."

"I wasn't sure what your plans were, so I saved Gracie a spot at the day care, just in case."

His smile widened.

"So sue me, already," she snapped, looking increasingly flustered.

Sue her? He wanted to kiss her.

With effort, he restrained himself. He didn't want to scare the lady off, after all. As much as he recognized the strength of his own heart and wanted to propel their relationship into fast-forward, he coaxed himself to stay in check until he knew for certain she returned his feelings.

How he would know that, he hadn't a clue. He didn't have much experience in reading women's emotions; he gave himself a mental tug backward.

Somehow, he encouraged himself, he would instinctively know when the time was right for him to speak. And this wasn't it.

Yet.

He shoved his hands in his pockets and rocked back on his heels, mentally distancing himself from the captivating woman before him. He tried to speak, but his words came out hoarse and raspy.

He cleared his throat and tried again. "Is tomorrow too soon?"

Jess shook her head.

"I thought I would talk to Vince and then go into Boulder to order materials for the fireplace. I don't know how long it will take me."

"It doesn't matter," she assured him, her big brown eyes glowing incandescently. "Tomorrow would be just perfect."

Jessica seated herself on a rocking chair in the corner of the day care nursery, tucked Gracie onto her lap, and then coaxed the warm bottle of formula into the baby's mouth. She smiled as Gracie reached out and propped the bottle with her own little fists.

Gracie was not only pulling herself up to a standing position when she was in her crib, but she was starting to show some manual dexterity, as well.

Babies grew into little girls too quickly, Jessica thought, with a mixture of joy and downheartedness. It would not be long now before Nate was chasing Gracie all over the mountain.

If he was around that long. She had so hoped that when he'd said he'd made some decisions, that he had meant he was going to stay at Morningway Lodge.

But he hadn't said that.

As she stared down at the sweet baby who'd completely won her heart, melancholy washed over her in black waves. She wondered if she'd get to see Gracie walking and talking and growing into a busy toddler.

She hoped so. With her whole heart, she wanted them to stay.

And if she were being honest, it wasn't just Gracie she would miss when they left. There was Nate to think of, as well.

Strong, charming, honorable Sergeant Morningway.

She smiled tenderly when she thought of Nate. He'd

been so convinced that he was going to run into resistance when he'd approached his brother with the fireplace idea, and had been genuinely astonished when Vince gave him—albeit grudgingly, Nate had assured her—consent to do the work.

And so for the past three weeks he had been dropping Gracie off at the day care early every weekday morning and taking off to work on his new project. He had the unfettered enthusiasm of a little boy in a toy shop. It was, Jessica mused, quite contagious. She couldn't seem to stop smiling these days, what with Nate running energetic mental circles around her.

She couldn't even really say it surprised her that he'd made it a practice to seek her out after hours as well. The fact that she visited his cabin as often as he came to hers was beside the point.

When Nate and Gracie weren't around, her life seemed conspicuously empty and quiet. While she used to consider the silence as a measure of her serenity, it was now a constant aching reminder of the past, and she found herself counting the minutes until she would see Nate and Gracie again.

They'd fallen into a comfortable routine. Nate picked her up in the morning, saying it was silly to drive two cars when he was headed in the direction of the day care anyway. Then, when he picked Gracie up in the evening, he waited around to drive Jessica home.

It only seemed fair that if he was going to ferry her about, the least she could do was cook him dinner. And then the next evening, he'd reciprocated, fixing her a killer omelet for supper. One evening led to another, and before Jessica realized it, the pattern had been set.

Much to her surprise, Nate had even accepted her invitation to accompany her to church the previous Sunday. She didn't know why she had felt compelled to ask him at all, given that he was not a religious man, and she certainly hadn't expected him to agree.

Now she wondered if he might not start attending church with her on a regular basis. And what, if anything, that meant about his relationship with God.

Speaking of Nate, she thought as she brought Gracie up to her shoulder for a burp, where was the man? She had expected him to arrive to take her home by the time she had finished feeding Gracie her bottle, but he was apparently running late.

When another half hour quietly passed and Nate still hadn't come to pick her up, Jessica started to worry in earnest.

Had something happened to him? Had there been an accident, maybe?

He'd told her that morning that he was going to be working on the roof today, building a chimney. What if he'd slipped and fallen?

She chastised herself for being a silly goose and turned her attention to Gracie.

"Hey, baby girl," she said, brushing her fingers through Gracie's soft curls, "what do you say we have a little fun with your hair?"

Gracie clearly didn't think that Jessica gathering her curls into a sprout on the top of her head and weaving a rubber band around it qualified as *fun*. She squawked and she wiggled and she even tried to slide off Jessica's lap, but Jessica just laughed and followed her movements until she'd achieved the look she desired.

How delightful Gracie looked bobbing her head with the little ponytail in place on top. That was why little girls were so much fun, Jessica thought, at once happy and sad. It was fun to play with their hair and dress them up in plush velvet and sparkly red shoes.

There were so many things she missed about Elizabeth, and so many more she would never see.

Jessica shook herself mentally, not wanting to entertain her morose feelings any further. Gracie was here in front of her, and that was all that mattered. Time moved so quickly. She needed to grasp the moment and live for *now*.

Sitting cross-legged on the indoor-outdoor carpet that covered the day care floor, Jessica willed her mind into the present, where Gracie was merrily pounding away on a toy xylophone and singing in a language all her own.

How could Jessica not find joy as she interacted with baby Gracie?

But when yet another half hour had passed, she decided it was time for action. She didn't have her SUV with her, but the day care van, complete with a car seat, was parked behind the building and she had the keys.

Without letting herself think too much about it, she bundled Gracie up and headed for the main lodge. Nate had no doubt simply lost track of the time, but she couldn't wait another second to know for sure.

She tried to remain calm, telling herself not to panic for no good reason, but to no avail.

Despite her best efforts, she mentally worked herself

into such a state as she drove that she half expected to see an ambulance in front of the lodge, or at the very least a crowd of concerned onlookers; but upon approaching, the lodge was as quiet as ever, and Nate's Jeep was parked in the front lot.

She breathed a sigh of relief, mentally chastising herself for her own stupidity. It wasn't like her to let her imagination run away with her.

With Gracie in her arms, she beelined for Jason Morningway's room.

When she knocked, it was Nate's smooth baritone that bid her to enter, and it was his beaming gaze that caught her eye the moment she stepped into the room.

Nate was sitting at the dining table with his father, a soda in his hand.

"Jess!" he exclaimed, bounding toward her and giving her an enthusiastic hug before sweeping Gracie into his arms. "What a surprise. What are you doing here? Is something the matter?"

Jessica arched an eyebrow and pointedly looked at her watch.

Nate looked at his own watch and then back at her, his expression genuinely surprised.

Jessica laughed. "So you lost track of the time, did you?"

He hung his head in mock shame, but he was still smiling. "I did. And I left you stranded and starving, no doubt. And speaking of stranded—how did you get to the lodge?"

"Compliments of the day care van," she answered, and then looked over his shoulder at the mostly finished fireplace. Nate had built it against the outside wall in gray stone. Though brand-new, it had an aged quality about it that Jessica recognized as exceptionally superior workmanship.

"Oh, Nate," she exclaimed, clapping her hands in delight. "It's gorgeous!"

"If not yet fully functional," he added with a grin. "Soon, though, Pop. I promise."

"You don't hear me complaining," Jason said, wheeling his chair around to face them. "I'm just enjoying your company. Now hand me my little granddaughter so I can give her a kiss."

Nate laughed and handed Gracie off to his father. "You got it, Pop. Hey...look at that, why don't you?"

He tapped his finger against Gracie's little sprout of a ponytail and laughed as it bounced. "Oh, man. Now that is what this little girl is missing, having to stay with a grumpy old marine. I'm never going to be able to do the hair thing with her. It's a good thing she's got you around for a female influence, Jess."

Jessica's heart welled as she watched the scene unfold and ingested Nate's compliment to her. Gracie's presence took years off Jason's features, and Nate's eyes were glowing with pride and joy.

Nate squeezed her shoulder. "How about I follow you back to the day care so you can drop off the van, and then I can take you home?"

Jessica nodded. "That sounds good to me. I'm starving."

"And I'm cooking," he assured her with a grin. "It's the least I can do to make up for the way I abandoned you like that."

Jason laughed along with Jessica.

"Okay, Pop," Nate said, scooping Gracie back into

his arms. "I'll be back first thing tomorrow morning to keep working on the fireplace."

"You take good care of that baby girl. And that lovely lady," Jason teased with a wink.

Jessica blushed.

Nate chortled and swung Gracie into the air, making her squeal with delight. "You can count on it."

"C'mon," Nate said as he and Jessica exited his father's apartment. "Let's go out the side door. I have something I want to show you."

Once outside, he reached for her hand and practically dragged her to the corner of the building. His enthusiasm was absolutely contagious, Jessica thought, laughing aloud as she jogged beside him. He was definitely unlike any other man she'd ever known, a delightful cross of all man and little boy.

"I've set the pipes for the flue," he explained, pointing toward the roof. "Now I'm working on stoning off the chimney. After that, all that's left for me to do is call in the county inspector to make sure everything is up to code. Then Pop can stoke it as high as he wants and enjoy the heat."

"And the view," Jessica added. "The fireplace is just beautiful, Nate. You did a fantastic job. I know your father appreciates it."

Gracie squealed and clapped her hands together as if in agreement.

Jessica giggled and pointed to the baby. "See? Even Gracie thinks so."

Nate's eyes warmed with pride.

"My girls," he said huskily. "I don't know how I ever got along without you two."

His words had an immediate effect on Jessica, who

felt heat flooding her face. Her throat constricted and burned until she was dizzy with the need for air. And it didn't help her one bit that Nate's gaze never left her face. She probably would have passed out cold right there on the spot had Gracie not distracted them both.

The baby clapped again, her little hands missing each other as often as they connected. She bounced in Nate's arms, her legs pumping in excitement.

"Da-da!" she crowed triumphantly.

Nate held the baby at arm's length, looking at her in amazement, his jaw literally dropping.

"Did you hear that?" he asked Jessica, his voice hoarse with emotion.

"Da-da," Gracie repeated, as if making certain Nate had, in fact, heard what he'd thought he'd heard. "Da-da-da-da-da-da."

Jessica knew Gracie was simply testing out her consonants, but her timing couldn't have been any better. Sure, the baby may not yet have connected the words to the person, but it was the adult response that would teach her what the words meant. And Jessica couldn't imagine anything taking the moment away from the beaming new father.

"I think she's proud of you, too, Da-da," Jessica said, excitement threading through her voice.

"Da-da," Nate repeated, wonder in his voice. "Her first word was Da-da."

"Well, of course it was, silly," she said, laughing at Nate's astonished expression. "What else would it be? You are the center of her little world, you know."

Hugging Gracie close, he whooped in delight and then reached for Jessica, fastening his arm around her waist and dragging her against him. He lifted her clear off her feet and swung her round and round.

Talk about being swept off her feet! It was Jessica's last conscious thought.

She laughed. Gracie laughed.

And Nate froze, his grip loosening enough for Jessica to find her footing. She was glad he continued to prop her up by his side, or she thought she might have melted right into the ground.

And then she looked up.

The smile on Nate's face faded and his eyes grew warm and golden. His free hand slid up her arm and splayed across her cheek.

"Jess?" His voice was husky, the word hovering somewhere between a question and a statement.

Jessica couldn't have answered him if her life had depended on it. Nor could she help her response, which was more natural even than breathing. She tipped up her chin and leaned in to him, an infinitesimal movement, but laced with meaning.

It was all the answer he needed.

Ever so slowly, he tilted his head to one side and brushed his lips over hers. It was the softest, briefest butterfly-wings of a kiss, but it sent Jessica over the moon and back again.

In that moment, she forgot all the reasons why this couldn't—and shouldn't—happen.

There was just Nate—his glowing eyes, his warm breath, his strong arms.

She wanted this. She wanted to be right here, right now, with this man. Tomorrow would be soon enough for regret.

He might have pulled back, but Jessica clutched onto his shirtfront and drew him forward.

That was all it took. He smiled, tunneled his fingers through her hair and kissed her again.

Just as their lips met for the second time, Jessica felt another hand in her hair. Gracie bunched up her little fist and pulled, and then laughed as if she understood her own joke.

Still locked warmly within their circle of three, Jessica and Nate laughed right along with her.

Chapter Ten

Nate's world was in overdrive, and all because of one little kiss. Okay, so maybe technically he'd gone in for seconds, but who could blame him.

Jess certainly had him off-kilter. He was a man who liked to act, not sit around mulling over his emotions. Yet here he was, checking and rechecking his handiwork on the chimney, knowing he ought to be concentrating solely on the final test to come and on whether or not this *project* of his was actually going to work and not smoke out the entire lodge.

He knew he should be nervous.

Instead, he was thinking about how similar his current emotions, those he experienced whenever he was with Jess, were to those of when he'd first received guardianship of Gracie.

Overwhelmed.

Confused.

Was this what it felt like to be in love?

He wished Ezra were here. He would know what Nate should do, or at least he would have had his back, leaving Nate feeling less exposed and vulnerable.

He remembered back to when Ezra first met Tamyra. Up until that day, Ezra had been a committed bachelor, just as Nate was. And then suddenly his friend was out to conquer the world, and he'd had the energy and confidence to back that up.

It had come, Nate knew, from the love of a good woman. Tamyra changed Ezra's whole outlook.

Ezra would have added his renewed faith in God, which seemed to go hand in hand with Ezra and Tamyra's deepening relationship. At the time, Nate had chalked it up to a man molding his life to please a woman, but now he was not so sure.

Had there been more to Ezra's faith? Was that what his friend had been trying to tell him?

Nate ran his fingers along the edge of the dried cement all around the stones, making sure there were no cracks in his handiwork.

For his part, Nate had teased Ezra unmercifully, and he'd certainly never understood what had come over his friend, not only to give up his bachelor freedom, but to step into the heavy-duty responsibility of being an active-duty marine, a husband and, eventually, a father.

There was a good reason Nate had never pursued a serious relationship with a woman, for who would willingly want to take on the life of a military spouse? He wouldn't have wished that on any of the women he'd dated over the years, and so he'd kept things simple, and the women at arm's length.

Or at least he'd *thought* that was the reason he'd remained emotionally distant.

Until now.

Until Jess.

Maybe the honest truth was he'd just never met the right woman—a woman who not only turned his head, but his heart.

Nate climbed down the ladder, only half aware when his feet met solid ground. With a grunt, he collapsed the twelve-foot ladder and carried it to the back of the building, where lodge guests wouldn't accidentally trip over it in their comings and goings. He would have put the ladder away, but the toolshed was already full to overflowing, and he thought he'd probably need it to climb back on the roof for the county inspection.

Funny, but now that he'd been thrust into a role of responsibility for another person, an unexpected new father figure for baby Gracie, becoming a family man didn't seem so bad.

Overwhelming, to be sure.

But not bad.

He'd never imagined that having someone depending on him for his well-being would feel so—*good*.

And never, ever, in a million years would he have imagined he could love someone as much as he did that baby girl.

If only his relationship with Jess was as straightforward and uncomplicated as his relationship with Gracie. He had less trouble reading Gracie's mind than he did trying to figure out what Jess was thinking.

He let himself into his father's apartment without knocking. These days, Pop anticipated his visits, and Nate certainly enjoyed spending time with his father. If he wasn't mistaken, it seemed to him that Pop was getting stronger and healthier by the day, a fact that Nate thanked God for.

"When are you going to bring my little granddaughter

around again?" his father asked as Nate fiddled with the flue to the chimney. He'd done quite a bit of construction on the lodge when he was a boy, but building this fireplace for his father had been a new kind of challenge. He wanted it to be just perfect when the inspector came.

"The county inspector comes out tomorrow," he said aloud. "I'd like to invite Jess to be here, so maybe I'll bring Gracie along as well."

Pop crowed happily. "You do that. I can't get enough of her. You know I have a God-given responsibility to spoil that baby girl."

Nate chuckled and shook his head. "I'll keep that in mind."

He turned to face his father, who cocked his right. eyebrow at him. With the way the left side of his face sagged from nerve damage, it gave his pop kind of a comical look.

"What?" Nate asked.

"You," his father replied sagely. "You look different."

Nate gazed down at his jeans and olive-green T-shirt, the same as he always wore. He shrugged. "I don't know what's different."

Pop guffawed loudly. "Not your clothes, boy. Your face."

Nate instinctively ran a hand across his cheek, noting the stubble. Other than the fact that he needed to shave, he couldn't feel any difference. "What's wrong with my face?"

"How is Jessica doing?" Pop asked, ostensibly changing the subject.

"Jess? She's fine. Why?"

Pop crowed again and pointed at Nate as if in accusation. "I knew it! I *knew* it! You're walking around with your head in the clouds, boy. There's only one thing that can put such a gleam in a man's eye, and that's a good woman."

Nate spent exactly two seconds thinking about trying to talk his father out of his fanciful notion, and then decided it wasn't worth the effort. Pop was dead-on with his assumption, and anything Nate could think of to say would only confirm it and subject him to an even worse bout of teasing.

Better just to remain silent.

He turned back to the fireplace and grunted. "Shall we light her up?"

Pop chuckled. "By all means. Let's see if a bomb defuser can build something up as well as he takes things apart."

Nate stiffened, feeling that his father was talking about more than just the new fireplace. Nate had torn down his share of family relationships over the years.

But Pop was still chuckling, so Nate let it go. He placed a couple of logs he'd cut earlier in the fireplace, and then added some old newspaper for kindling, pushing the wadded-up paper into the cracks between the logs.

"Ready?" he asked, glancing over his shoulder as he fished in his pocket for a pack of matches.

Pop beamed and nodded.

Nate struck a match and lit the crumpled newsprint in several places, blowing on the small flames to add more oxygen. After a moment, the wood caught fire, and soon there was a warm, snapping blaze.

Still crouched before the fireplace, Nate leaned on his elbows and stared intently at the crackling flames, thinking how the golden warmth reflected what he was feeling in his heart.

Life was good.

Better every day, in fact. He couldn't help but send up another silent thank-you to God. He seemed to be doing a lot of that lately, he realized.

Pop wheeled his chair up next to Nate and laid a hand on his shoulder.

"It's wonderful," Pop said in a hushed tone.

"Yeah, Pop," Nate agreed in the same quiet, reverent tone of voice. "It is."

Nate bounded forward with the most adorable combination of anxiety and youthful anticipation that Jessica simply didn't have the will to resist him when he showed up at her cabin an hour before she was due at the day care and asked her to spend the day with him while the county inspector looked over his handiwork.

The day care wasn't at full capacity today, and she knew the other teachers could handle the children. Besides, Nate had coerced her with the knowledge that Jason Morningway wanted to spend some time with Gracie, and Nate would, he wryly pointed out, be too busy with the inspection to keep an eye on the baby.

She felt decidedly awkward after the kiss she'd shared with Nate, but he wasn't treating her any differently than he ever had, so she forced herself to relax and go with the flow, mentally denying the intimacy she was feeling in her heart.

Could she put the past behind her and forge her

future with Nate? Her stomach clenched just thinking about it.

Eventually, she would have to face what she was walking headlong into. She would have to put a label on them. She would have to crawl off the fence she'd been straddling since the day she'd met Nate and Gracie and declare a side.

But not today.

This day belonged to Nate, and Jessica wanted to be by his side as he triumphed over the skeletons in his own closet.

She didn't protest when he took her hand to help her out of his Jeep, nor when he hitched Gracie to his other side and laced his fingers through Jessica's. He was looking for support, she reasoned; and after all, that was what she was there for.

The county inspector, who introduced himself as Michael Sheridan, was waiting for Nate in the dayroom, sitting on the sofa and consulting his clipboard.

She and Nate ushered Michael into Jason's apartment and the inspection began. Giving Jessica's hand one last squeeze, Nate slipped Gracie into her arms and turned his attention to Michael Sheridan's questions. Not wanting to be in the way, Jessica hurried to Jason's side and propped the baby in his lap.

She watched the inspection from a distance, her attention slipping back and forth between Nate and Michael, and Jason and Gracie.

To her surprise, Jason slowly lifted his left arm and crooked it to give Gracie a better seat on his lap. The strain on his face told her what kind of effort he was expending, but the results were astonishing.

"Why, sir," she exclaimed. "You're moving your left arm!"

Jason grinned widely and winked at her.

"Call me Jason, please. And yes, I'm getting limited movement back in my arm. My leg is still giving me problems, but my physical therapist is hopeful I'll regain some sensation there."

"That's wonderful news!"

"Rosemary, my physical therapist, is a real drill sergeant. She doesn't let me get away with anything, and she is constantly pushing me to work beyond what I think I can do."

"Sounds like she's doing her job," Jessica teased, punctuating her sentence with a chuckle as she slid into a chair across from Jason and leaned forward. Nate was leading Michael outside, so she turned her full attention to Jason and Gracie.

"And this little one," he continued, kissing Gracie on the forehead, "has turned the word *motivation* right on its ear."

"She does that, doesn't she?" Jessica queried softly, reaching her index finger out so the baby could clasp it. "She's turned all of our lives inside out."

Jason chuckled. "Only Gracie?"

Her gaze snapped to the old man, who was grinning at her like the cat who had eaten the proverbial canary.

Jessica felt her skin burning from the tips of her toes to the top of her head, and knew she must be blushing a frightful color of red.

"So I take it from your reaction that my son is getting to you, as well?"

Jessica rocked back in her chair as if he'd physically

pushed her there. He hadn't touched her with more than his words, of course. It was a good thing, too, Jessica thought. If he so much as grazed her with his pinky finger, she would no doubt fall to the floor.

"I— He—" she stammered, but couldn't seem to get her mouth to form a single coherent word for the life of her.

And what would she say, anyway?

How could she deny what was clearly written all over her face, at least if Jason's gleeful chuckle was anything to go by.

Jason patted her knee reassuringly. "There, there, dear. I apologize. I didn't mean to embarrass you. This old man just doesn't know when to keep his opinion to himself."

"It's not that," she assured him, sweeping in a giant breath of air in order to keep herself from feeling that a noose was tightening around her neck. "I just—it's just that I'm a little confused right now."

"Of course you are," Jason agreed with a knowing nod, now laughing heartily.

Gracie stared up at her grandfather a moment with wide, startled eyes, and then flapped her arms and squealed happily, catching Jason's excitement.

Jessica stared at the baby and tried desperately to regain her equilibrium. *Confused* didn't even begin to cover what she was feeling.

Jason winked. "I still remember how completely out of my head I was when I fell in love with Nate's mother. It was a disconcerting feeling, to say the least."

Jessica dragged her gaze away from Gracie and centered it on Jason. The choking sensation had returned with reinforcements.

Fall in love?

Was that what she was doing?

There was no denying her strong attraction for Nate, or how empty her little cabin felt whenever he and Gracie weren't present.

But *love?* Did she even dare think of the word in context with Nate Morningway?

The L word, her friends in high school used to call it. *First comes love, then comes marriage, then comes the baby in the baby carriage.*

Only this time the baby had come first. But that didn't make what she felt for Nate any less real or tangible. If anything, it only added to the joy she felt whenever she was around the two of them.

And the confusion.

Because she could never forget—not for one second—that she had already been around this particular block once, and with disastrous results.

A shattered heart. A broken home.

A husband who didn't mean his wedding vows for forever.

Even with the faith in God she now held dear to her heart, there were no guarantees in life. Her destination was assured, but the road getting there could be bumpy, and she knew that better than anyone.

If she gave her heart to Nate, she risked having it broken all over again. It had taken her two years to even begin to recover from her last relationship. She might never recover from another bad experience.

"Are you okay?" Jason asked, breaking into her thoughts.

"Huh?" she asked, dazed. "Oh. Yes. Everything is fine."

Jason looked deeply into her eyes and shook his head. "I don't think so."

Jessica didn't know the words to say to put Jason's mind at ease. *Her* mind wasn't at ease. And somehow she could tell Jason knew that.

But as it happened, she didn't have the opportunity to say anything, as Nate burst back into the room, followed by Michael Sheridan, who was still scribbling notes on his clipboard.

"Light the fire," Michael said, tapping the point of his pen against the clipboard.

Nate winked at Jessica as he moved to the fireplace to do as he was bid. Jessica smiled to herself. Apparently all was well with the inspection. She was glad, for Nate's sake.

After a few more minutes, the inspector announced that he was finished, and he complimented Nate on a job well done.

Nate beamed. Jason chuckled under his breath.

Jessica wondered if Jason understood just how important it was for Nate to complete this project for his father. She thought, gazing at Jason's bright gray eyes, that he probably did.

"Jess and I will walk you out," Nate told Michael. He moved to Jessica's chair and held out a hand to her. "You'll be okay with Gracie for a few minutes, won't you, Pop?"

Jason chuckled. "Take all the time you need. My little granddaughter and I are doing just fine here all by ourselves."

Jessica accepted Nate's hand, and wasn't really surprised when he didn't let it go after she'd stood. Despite her mixed feelings, it felt *right* to be linked with Nate in such a natural way.

Together, they walked the inspector outside. Jessica heard the sound of a table saw splitting wood the moment they walked out the door, and absently wondered where it came from.

As soon as they stepped off the porch, she saw the source of the sound. Vince was at the far side of the lodge, dressed in jeans and a denim shirt that Jessica thought looked odd on a man who usually wore a suit, despite the fact that they were at a mountain retreat. A backward-facing baseball cap covered his hair.

Looming behind Vince was the project he was clearly working on. He had framed in what looked like was going to be a good-size shed and was now cutting plywood to attach to the two-by-fours.

Nate lifted his free arm and waved to Vince, who just stared back at the small group, his arms propped on his hips, his posture suggesting they'd somehow interrupted his work. Still, Jessica was proud of Nate for trying, even when Vince didn't respond positively.

Nate's movement caught the inspector's attention, and he looked to where Vince was building. His gaze narrowed as he crooked a hand over his forehead to block the glare of the sunshine so he could see better.

"Who is that?" Michael asked.

"My brother, Vince," Nate answered cordially. "He runs Morningway Lodge."

"I see," Michael muttered, tapping his pen on his clipboard for a moment before moving decisively in Vince's direction.

Nate flashed Jessica a surprised look before following the inspector to where Vince was working.

"Vince, this is county inspector Michael Sheridan. He's come to look over the fireplace I built."

Vince wiped his palms against his jeans and then held out a hand to Michael.

"I assume you have a permit to build here?" Michael asked, looking over Vince's shoulder and gesturing toward the frame of the shed.

Vince's gaze widened, and he shook his head. "No, sir. It's just a shed. My old one is full to overflowing with tools. I thought I'd better get another one up before winter hits us hard. It's not a big building project or anything."

"Even so," Michael continued, "you will need to have a permit to build."

Vince looked flustered. And frustrated. Jessica squeezed Nate's hand, wondering if he might be able to say something—anything—to diffuse the situation. She felt Nate tense, but he remained silent.

"Is this a new law?" Vince asked. "I don't recall my father getting permits to build. And this is private property."

"I realize that," Michael said, his voice a clipped, businesslike monotone. "And yes, the law is new—at least relative to the age of your property. Still, the fees must be paid in to our office before you can continue with your work here."

"I see," Vince said, not sounding happy about it at all, and Jessica couldn't blame him. He had enough to worry about without having to jump through extra hoops to complete a simple project. "In that case, I'll see to getting a permit right away."

"I'm afraid I'm going to have to insist that it be done immediately," Michael informed him, his voice and expression neutral. "If not, you will be fined for building without a permit. I warn you now, the fine is pretty steep."

"You'd fine me over one shed?" Vince snapped, then pinched his lips together and frowned.

"That's the way it works," the inspector insisted. "I don't make the rules, but I do have to enforce them."

"Yes, sir. Of course. I understand, and I'll see to it right away."

"All right, then. I'll expect to see you in my office immediately, so we can clear up this paperwork."

Vince nodded, his face still strained, but the inspector had already turned to Nate.

"Mr. Morningway," Michael said, shaking Nate's hand. "It's been a pleasure."

"Thank you, sir," Nate responded. His voice was coarse and cracking, and Jessica knew he was struggling merely to speak. She squeezed his hand again as Michael got into his vehicle and turned off down the unpaved road.

Nate immediately turned to Vince, his arm outstretched in supplication. "Hey, I'm sorry about that, bro. I didn't realize that—"

Vince whirled on him, his sizzling scowl bringing Nate's words to an instant stop.

"Well done, little brother," Vince said, his voice sharp with sarcasm. "You've really gone and done it this time, haven't you?"

Chapter Eleven

Though Vince hadn't moved from where he'd been standing, Nate felt as though his brother had sucker punched him right in his gut. He stiffened to keep from clutching at his midsection.

"What did *I* do?" Nate knew his question sounded defensive. It was. And it was the wrong question to ask. He already knew Vince was going to blame him for whatever inconvenience he would face.

"If they slap me with a fine because of this stupid permit business it's going to be on your head. I have to meet with suppliers in Denver this week, so I'm not going to be able to get it right away. Thanks a lot, Nate."

Nate dropped Jess's hand and took an unconscious step backward, as if reeling from a blow. He felt the overwhelming urge to come out swinging, to settle their differences the way they had as children.

He hoped he'd matured a little bit in ten years, and with effort, he unclenched his fists. Still, he couldn't let it completely go. "How is it my fault you didn't get a permit before you started building?"

Real mature, there, Morningway, he chastised himself. *Way to go.*

"I didn't know I was supposed to get a permit for a measly shed," Vince barked. "Pop never needed a permit to build."

"Look," Nate said, holding out his hands in a placating manner. "I just wanted to do this fireplace thing on the up-and-up. It's been years since I've built anything. I had to make sure it was safe, for Pop's sake. You wouldn't have wanted me accidentally burning down the lodge, now would you?"

Nate scowled, hating the feeling he had to justify his actions to his brother. Vince glowered back at him, which didn't help matters at all.

"Sure. Make me look like the bad guy."

Nate opened his mouth, then snapped it closed again. Of all the pigheaded, irrational—

He jumped, startled, when Jess placed her hand on his arm. When he'd started butting heads with his brother, he'd almost forgotten she was there. Guilt and humiliation flooded through him, raw and stinging. It was bad enough that Vince thought him every kind of fool without having Jess as an audience.

"We need to go get Gracie," she said, her voice low and even, as if she hadn't just witnessed the juvenile scene in front of her. "Despite what he said, your father isn't up to watching her for an extended period of time. He's still so weak, and you know how wiggly she gets when she has to sit still too long."

Nate sighed, the anger draining from him. Jess was right. And more than that, she was clearly giving him a way out of his latest confrontation with Vince.

Vince shrugged and waved his arm in what Nate thought was a condescending manner.

"Go get your baby," Vince snapped. "But this isn't over between us, bro. Not even close."

Nate thought it the best part of valor not to respond at all, so he turned and stalked away, hearing Jess's murmur of surprise and her quick steps after him.

In record time, he said goodbye to his father and bundled Gracie in her car seat in the back of the Jeep, all the while not speaking to Jess at all. Wisely, Nate thought, she didn't try to strike up any kind of conversation with him, either, but simply buckled herself in and waited. He was in no mood for small talk, and he *sure* didn't want to talk about the humiliating incident between he and Vince.

Jess didn't speak until he had parked the Jeep in front of her cabin. Nate clutched the steering wheel as she opened the car door, but she didn't immediately disembark as he expected. If he had been in her position, he'd be running for cover right about now, fearing an imminent explosion.

Out of the corner of his eye, he could see that she'd turned toward him and was quietly searching his expression, but he just stared straight ahead, knowing he was glowering. Though it was unfair, he couldn't seem to be able to put a lid on his anger, even for Jess's sake.

"Are you okay?" she asked at last, her voice quivering with emotion.

Nate pinched his lips together and said nothing, afraid if he did he would bark at her.

"Vince was caught off guard," she explained, hesitating, her big brown eyes widening, when Nate's gaze snapped to hers. "Give him some time to think it through, and I'm sure he'll see reason."

"Why should he? He's right and he knows it," Nate growled sharply, then squeezed his hands on the steering wheel, angry at himself for lashing out at Jess. None of this was her fault. She was trying to be supportive, and he knew it.

"He's had a lot of time to think about my coming back home," he said, softening his tone. "All I've done is cause him problems since I've been here. This is just the icing on the cake."

Jess reached out and touched his shoulder, but he shrugged it off.

"You know that's not true," she pleaded. "Whether Vince wants to admit it right now or not, you've been a great help to him—and to your father. Jason is enjoying a warm fire as we speak because of all the hard work that you've done."

Nate snorted. "Pop is going to hear about this. What is he going to think of me interfering? Morningway Lodge is his baby. His dream. And now I've gone and made things more complicated for him by not thinking things through."

"Take a deep breath, Nate," Jessica suggested softly. "It isn't your fault Vince didn't get a permit. You followed the law, which was the right thing to do. Vince will realize that, too, once he's had time to cool off. I'm sure he wasn't trying to do anything illegal, so in the long run, this can only help him."

"Not if they slap a huge fine on him," Nate grated, his forehead aching from his deepening scowl.

"That doesn't have to happen, now does it? I mean,

all the inspector said was that he has to go get a permit to build. How is that so bad?"

Nate shrugged. Jess was right. It wasn't an insurmountable difficulty, just an extra hoop to jump through.

Except…

"I don't know for sure, but I get the impression Vince doesn't have a lot of working capital. Morningway Lodge was built as a ministry, not to make a lot of money."

"Then I'll pay for it," Jessica stated, nodding and smiling as she warmed to the idea. "I have some money tucked away in my savings account that we can use to get Vince his permit."

Nate's gaze widened, and he surprised himself that his jaw didn't drop. His pulse pounded in his temple. "You'd do that for Vince?"

Her gaze widening, she shook her head. "Not for Vince. For you."

Nate tried to swallow around the raw lump of emotion burning in his throat.

"I'll do it," he said. "But I don't need your money. I have some savings of my own."

"Okay," she agreed with a gentle smile. "I'm sure Vince will appreciate it."

Nate barked out a dry laugh. "I don't know about that. But I'll sure feel better."

"And now that you're finished with the fireplace, maybe you could assist Vince in building his shed. You can't depend on the weather in Colorado to stay nice in October, and he'll need all the help he can get."

"Maybe," Nate agreed, but his mind was already

migrating to more pleasant thoughts than trying to work things out with Vince.

Like how wise and thoughtful Jess was.

And how beautiful.

And how he didn't know if he could ever get along without her.

He felt closer to Jess in that one instant than he'd ever felt to another human being. His mind stuttered over the words to tell her what he was thinking, but they just wouldn't come out of his mouth.

What a time to get tongue-tied, when it suddenly seemed so monumentally important for her to understand how he felt, how much she meant to him.

"Jess, I—" he started, only to stumble to a stop. The awkward silence loomed before him in the air, feeling very much like that breath-holding moment when he was about to disarm a bomb, knowing that the slightest false move would cause it to blow up in his face.

Only this time he wasn't working to save the lives of others. It was his own heart on the line.

"Nate?" she asked, her voice full of concern.

He turned as much as his large body would allow within the confines of his seat. The steering wheel bit into his side, but he didn't really care.

The only thing that mattered was this moment.

This woman.

When she reached for the door handle, Nate put out his hand to stop her. Their fingers met, and the electricity between them was palpable.

"Jess," he said again, but when no more words came, he simply took her in his arms. He might not be able to tell her how he felt, he thought as he drew her to him, so close that their breath intermingled, but he could certainly show her.

With a groan that came from deep in his chest, he slanted his head and centered his mouth over hers. Her lips were soft and pliant, and without conscious thought, he deepened the kiss.

She was so sweet and giving. He heard her murmur as she clutched her fists into the lapel of his bomber jacket, but he didn't know what it was that she said, if it had been real words at all.

Time ceased to have meaning. There was only Jess. Sweet, wonderful Jess.

"Nate."

He loved the sound of his name on her lips.

"Nate, stop."

It was only then that he realized she was no longer clutching at his jacket to pull him closer, but was pushing him away, her hands flat on his chest.

His mind was still reeling with the discovery of his feelings for Jess, but he didn't miss her troubled expression, nor the tears that welled up in her huge brown eyes, making their depth seem infinite.

He sat back, giving her the space she obviously needed. "What's wrong, honey?"

"I'm sorry, Nate," she choked out, scrubbing her palms across her eyes as if she were angry at her own tears, as if it was a show of weakness.

Nate didn't think there was anything weak about Jessica Sabin. She had a strength of character he could only hope to aspire to, and she had the kind of faith that could move mountains.

But he had clearly upset her with his actions, and he felt like a big oaf for not realizing it sooner. If she needed more time, he would certainly give it to her. He'd only wanted to express what was in his heart, not cause her any kind of distress.

"I'm sorry, Jess," he apologized, his voice low and gravelly.

"No," she replied, so softly he could barely hear the word. She had been looking down at her hands, which were clasped in her lap, but now she gazed up at him. "*I'm* the one who should apologize."

The sorrow in her gaze took his breath away. He mentally scrambled to figure out what he had done to make her react that way.

"What?" he asked at last, still clueless as to what he had done, and even more as to what he should say, only knowing he needed to do *something* to make things right between them.

"I—I'm really sorry, Nate," she stammered. "But things just cannot go on this way."

Without another word, and without giving him the opportunity to say anything—not that his cloudy mind could think of anything to say—she reached behind her for the door handle and scrambled out of the Jeep and into her cabin, slamming both the car door and the cabin door behind her as she went.

Nate didn't try to follow her, gathering himself up enough to realize he wouldn't accomplish anything by pushing her too hard. But he sat for a long time in front of her cabin, his arms crooked over the steering wheel and his head on his arm.

What was wrong?

How could he fix it?

Not knowing where else to turn, he began to pray.

"Dear God, if You are there, and Jess believes You are, please help me. Please."

Sitting in the corner easy chair with the lights off, Jessica chastised herself as every kind of fool. And the worst thing was, the only one she'd been fooling was herself.

How had she thought, after the first time Nate had kissed her, that they could continue on as friends? Something foundational had changed between them in that moment, and she had either failed to recognize it or, more likely, had simply shoved it to the back of her mind and refused to acknowledge it, hoping against hope it would go away on its own.

Like *that* was going to happen.

She was an idiot.

And now she had hurt Nate.

She'd seen the pain of her rejection in his eyes, and that was the very last thing she ever wanted to do. She remembered his expression when she'd made her escape, and it broke her heart.

Of course the man was confused by her sudden emotional turnaround. She had sent him every mixed signal in the book.

If only she was the sweet, innocent woman Nate thought her to be. If only she had half the strength Nate attributed to her.

The memory of his voice warmed her heart even now—the way he laughed, how he tenderly shortened her name to *Jess*. He was the only one who called her that, and oddly enough, it was rubbing off on her. She was beginning to think of herself by that nickname.

If only there was no past—only the present and the future.

But all the wishing in the world would not make it so. It was what it was, and it was high time she stopped ignoring the facts.

Why, oh, why had she not been honest with Nate from the beginning?

It wasn't as if she hadn't had plenty of opportunities to tell him the truth about her past. She'd just chosen *not* to, despite the fact that he had opened up to her early on in their relationship, and had trusted her with the depth of his secrets.

Yet she had remained silent. And look where that had gotten her.

All this time she'd been telling herself that she was protecting herself from heartbreak, and now she faced the truth.

No more excuses. She cared for Nate—and Gracie— very deeply. And that raised the stakes to intimidating odds.

How could she now bring her past into casual conversation? *Dinner was lovely, and by the way, I've been married before.*

No. That would never work.

What she needed to do, she realized, was to confront the whole situation head-on and tell him everything she'd been hiding. She couldn't go on living a lie.

She had to revisit her past, and take Nate along for the ride.

Yes. That was what she would do. She would talk to him.

But not now.

Nate was up to his ears with the situation with

Vince. Jessica thought it was best to give him time to work that out before she sprang anything new on him. He was in enough emotional turmoil without her adding dry kindling to the flame.

She wrapped a blanket around her legs and curled into the chair. She was no longer in denial, but she would put Nate's needs before her own.

It wouldn't be easy. She knew the next time she saw him, the weight of her decision would likely cause her to blurt it all out to him. And that was the last thing he needed right now.

Perhaps the best thing, for the time being, was not to see Nate at all.

Chapter Twelve

Nate had never been so frustrated in all his life. He was angry at himself for pushing Jess too far, too fast. In his rush to make his feelings known to her, he had trampled all over hers. He had clipped the wrong wire on the bomb and it had exploded.

He should have known better.

What concerned him most, however, was not the sad state of his own heart. It was Jess.

She was avoiding him.

At first, it had only been a suspicion on his part. He'd brought Gracie to the day care so he could go to Boulder to pursue getting the permit for Vince, and Jess had been nowhere to be found, even though her SUV was parked in the lot.

But what had started out as mere conjecture was now, in Nate's mind, an unavoidable fact. Not only was Jess not visible at the day care, but in the following week, she hadn't once called or come over.

And that wasn't like her.

No more shared dinners. No more quiet evenings. Nate was going out of his mind.

He could have sought her out, visited her cabin in the evening like he used to do. But if Jess was avoiding him—and she clearly was—it was for a reason. He hadn't a clue what that reason might be, but he sensed the right thing to do was give her the time and space she had asked for in her actions, if not with words.

But after an entire week of not seeing her pretty face, it was killing him to stay away. He didn't know how much more of this forced isolation he could take. It was sheer torture.

And because it was Saturday, he had nothing to do except think about it. Even caring for baby Gracie's needs didn't do more than mildly distract him.

It was still early morning, Nate realized when he glanced at his watch. How was he possibly going to make it through a whole, long empty weekend?

With Gracie fed and changed and now playing quietly in her playpen, Nate found himself pacing back and forth from the kitchen to the living room and back, feeling caged in by his own tiny cabin.

On his tenth trip from the kitchen to the front door, he finally decided he couldn't stand to be cooped up inside for another moment. He was so wound up mentally, and his muscles were so tense and tight, that he couldn't think straight.

"How about you and I go for a run, baby girl?" he asked Gracie, sweeping her into his arms and tossing her into the air. Her laughter echoed in the small cabin.

"I'll take that as a yes."

It only took him a minute to bundle Gracie up and prop her in the backpack. He was getting better at this baby stuff, he realized as he took off down the mountain path nearest to his cabin.

Now, if he could only adjust his learning curve with Jess. He knew it was pointless to beat himself up about it, but he felt as if he'd somehow failed in nearly every relationship in his life. He'd failed God. He'd failed his father, and then Vince.

And somehow, he'd failed Jess.

He'd been running down a little-used path, mulling over the situation with Jess, when she suddenly materialized in front of him.

At first he didn't believe his own eyes when she burst over a hill, her thick blond ponytail swinging behind her. Had he finally lost his mind completely, conjuring her up from some messed-up part of his brain?

But as she approached and slowed before him, he knew he wasn't dreaming.

She had obviously been running hard. Her face was flushed from exertion and she pinched at a stitch in her side as she struggled to slow down her labored breathing. Sweat poured from her brow, and wisps of hair that had escaped her ponytail framed her face. She looked like someone had sent her through a tumble cycle in a clothes dryer.

And Nate thought he'd never seen her look as beautiful as she did at this moment. Relief rushed through him at finally having the opportunity to see her face-to-face, just to be able to talk to her.

"Jess," he exclaimed, not able to keep the enthusiasm he was feeling from his voice. "I wondered when I would see you."

Jess's face showed a combination of shock and

panic. Her eyes were wide, and her nostrils flared. She reminded Nate of a cornered wild animal, and he thought she might bolt at any moment.

He couldn't let that happen.

His meeting with her in the woods like this was nothing short of divine intervention. Had God been listening to the prayers he'd uttered only with his heart?

"Did you get the permit?" she asked politely. Nate thought she sounded almost as if she were speaking to a stranger, not a man with whom she'd shared so much of her life, a man with whom she'd shared kisses.

"It took the better part of a week, but yeah, I did finally get it. I'm glad Vince was tied up in Denver or this never would have worked."

"I'm happy to hear it went well for you. What did Vince say when you told him?"

Nate shrugged. "I haven't told him yet."

He wanted to add that he'd waited because he'd hoped she would be with him when he told his brother the good news. She had more than a vested interest in this, after all. It had been her idea in the first place.

But she'd already flashed him a distant smile and was jogging in place.

"Good to see you," she murmured, and then pulled herself up as she started to jog by him.

Nate's hands snaked out of their own accord, blocking her way. He didn't know what to say, but he knew he had to keep her here with him, so he blurted out the prominent thought on his mind.

"Have you been avoiding me?"

It was a rhetorical question. Of course she'd been avoiding him. The question was, *why?*

As he hadn't given her room to run by him, she stopped and took two steps backward, crossing her arms in the age-old line of defense. He wanted to reach for her and erase the tension on her face, but he knew that was probably the last thing she would want him to do, so he jammed his hands in the pockets of his gray sweatpants.

Jess stared at him for a long moment without answering him.

"Does it matter?" she finally asked, her voice so low Nate could hardly hear the words.

Her question angered him. And flustered him. And frustrated him. His pulse pounded in his ears.

What did she mean, *does it matter?* Did she think he was stringing her along in some way, toying with her emotions?

"*You* matter," he replied gruffly. "Jess, what's wrong? Talk to me. Whatever is bothering you, we can work through it together. Just please don't shut me out of your life. Please."

The fight instantly went out of her, and she physically drooped before taking a seat on an old log that had fallen along the side of the path.

"Okay, Nate," she said softly. "You're right. It's time you knew the truth about me."

Jessica sighed and folded her hands in her lap. This confrontation was inevitable. She'd known that since the moment she'd walked out of Nate's embrace a week ago. But that didn't make it any easier.

How would she ever find the words to make Nate understand what she didn't really comprehend herself?

How could she tell him that she couldn't go forward without moving back?

"I think—" she started, and then stopped and cleared her throat. "That is, I—"

She stared down at her hands, unable to find the courage to look Nate straight in the eye. He crouched before her and gently lifted her chin with the crook of his knuckle.

"Know this," he whispered raggedly. "Whatever it is that you need to say to me, it won't change the way I feel about you."

Jessica wanted to exclaim in disbelief, but his warm, gold-flecked gaze stopped her. He really believed in what he was saying.

He believed in *her*.

And she trusted him. Not because she had to, or because he was pressuring her to come clean with whatever was bothering her.

She just *did*. When he smiled at her, she felt as if she could see right into his heart. And she liked what she viewed there.

"There are some things about my past I haven't told you about. Things that make me nervous about a new relationship."

Nate nodded. "I know. Go on."

"You know?"

Nate nodded again and smiled in encouragement. He brushed his thumb along her cheek. "Nothing specific, of course. But I've been around you long enough to know that something's been bothering you, and I'm glad you want to talk to me about it."

The deep end wasn't going to suddenly become shallow, no matter how much she wished it to be so.

Jessica swept in a breath to calm herself before she could speak, and then dove in. "I feel really close to you and Gracie."

"We like you, too, Jessica Sabin."

"That's just it," she muttered.

"What? I don't understand."

"Jessica Sabin is my married name."

Married? Jess was *married?*

Whatever Nate had thought she was going to tell him, this was not it. His heart dropped through his shoes and his mind struggled to catch up.

"I didn't know," he breathed raggedly.

He reached for her left hand, gently uncurling her fingers and staring down at them.

Just as he thought. No ring.

"You aren't wearing a wedding band," he pointed out softly.

"Oh, no. I'm not married *now,*" she clarified briskly. "I was married. It ended."

"I see," he said, although he wasn't really sure he did. He didn't know whether or not to be relieved at her words. "I'm sorry."

He was still struggling to mesh the mental picture he had with the Jess he knew with the woman who was sitting before him now, telling him she'd had a whole other life before him that he knew nothing about.

"I had a baby," she said, her voice cracking under the strain of emotion. "A baby girl. Her name was Elizabeth. Sweet baby Elizabeth."

Nate reached for her other hand and pressed them both to his lips, and then close to his heart. He couldn't bear to hear the agony in her voice. He wanted to erase the suffering from her countenance.

When she hurt, he hurt.

And he hadn't missed the tense she'd used in reference to her daughter. *Had* a baby. Her name *was*.

When she didn't elaborate, he slid onto the log beside her and put his arm around her shoulders. She had to know he would be there for her, no matter what.

Still secured in the backpack, Gracie hadn't hollered or squirmed, so he thought she must have fallen asleep as she usually did from the rhythmic rocking movement of his jog. He was glad for it, since at the moment, Jess required his full attention.

"Was?" he asked gently.

"Elizabeth was eight months old when she passed," she said, her breath ragged. "I put her to bed one night as always. I checked in on her before I went to sleep myself, and she was fine. When I woke up the next morning, she wasn't breathing."

"Crib death," Nate whispered. He'd heard of the horrible term, but had never known anyone who'd lost a child to it. He couldn't even begin to imagine losing Gracie that way. Even the thought of it sent sharp stabs of panic through his chest.

What kind of horror had Jess lived through?

"Oh, Jess. I'm sorry."

"SIDS." She shook her head. "It was the beginning of the end for me. Or at least that was how it felt at the time."

Nate pulled her closer, feeling that, if he let her go, she would simply disappear.

"I can't imagine what you've been through."

"And I can't even begin to describe it." She stared off into the distance, somewhere over Nate's left shoulder. "It was as if my grief for Elizabeth sucked the life right out of my body. I went through the motions of eating and sleeping, but my mind had retreated to somewhere deep inside me, somewhere where my sweet baby girl still lived. There was a big, black pit in my stomach. I kept waiting for it to grow smaller, but it never did."

Nate tenderly brushed a wisp of hair from her forehead. "That must have been awful."

His sympathy must have touched her heart, for tears sprang to her eyes and she quickly wiped them away.

"I still grieve for Elizabeth. Every single day. I miss her so much. But life keeps happening whether you are ready for it or not."

Nate knew the feeling. Ezra's death had been really hard on him, and Ezra was just a friend. If it hadn't been for the fact that he had Gracie to care for...

The baby, he realized, had been his lifeline during one of the toughest times in his life.

"How long has it been?" he asked gently and tentatively.

She sniffled. "Elizabeth would be nearly three years old now."

No amount of time would really be enough, Nate thought. Not ever. And her wounds were obviously still fresh—too fresh to talk about. At all.

How, he wondered, had he missed this deep of a dynamic in her life when he'd spent so much time with her?

Was he blind?

"And your husband?" he asked as an afterthought. "What happened to him?"

Jess looked away from him. "Russ didn't deal with his grief in the same way I did. I know I wasn't looking at things rationally at the time, but I just couldn't understand the way he wanted to throw himself back into normal life."

"He did that?" Anger at a man he'd never met surged through him. Jessica deserved strength and support from the man who'd vowed to cherish her, not rejection and abandonment.

"I've had a lot of time to contemplate what happened. I know now that he was grieving, just in a different way than me. But at the time it felt like he was in denial, that he had betrayed Elizabeth's memory. I thought he didn't even care that Elizabeth's life had been snuffed out so prematurely."

"I'm so sorry," Nate said again. He knew he was repeating himself, but he didn't know what else to say. He wished with all his heart he was better with words, that he could think of something to say that would bring her real comfort.

But of course he couldn't, so he simply continued to hold her while she sobbed, gently brushing away her tears with the pad of his thumb.

"Russ tried to find me in the dark space into which I'd retreated. He really did. But I was inconsolable, and he needed someone to be there for him, too.

"That person wasn't me. Couldn't be me. And so he left."

"He left you?" Nate's voice rose in pitch with every word. He tried and failed to contain the sudden surge of righteous indignation he felt toward Jess's ex-husband on her behalf.

What kind of a man would leave his wife when she had just lost a child?

"He needed someone," she explained matter-of-factly. "And I wasn't there for him. He found someone else who was."

Nate clenched his jaw. "I still don't understand how he could—"

Jess cut him off. "We were divorced by then. She got pregnant. Russ married her. Maybe out of a sense of obligation. Maybe because he fell in love with her."

Honor? That man didn't know the meaning of the word, Nate thought fiercely. An honorable man didn't abandon the woman he'd married when the going got tough. That wasn't love. "Of all the inconsiderate, stupid, selfish—"

She cut him off again, this time with a wave of her hand. "It's the past, Nate. I've set aside my anger toward him. In a way, I kind of understand why he did what he did."

"He had no right to hurt you that way. Not when you were already suffering. If he were here now, I'd give him a piece of my mind." *And my fist,* he added mentally, fuming so strongly he thought he must be having smoke come out of his ears.

"I'm over it," she snapped, her composure breaking as she broke into a new round of sobs.

No, she wasn't.

Nate couldn't see how. No wonder she'd balked at the thought of a new relationship. She must have trust issues a mile long. And rightly so.

If he could stand before Russ Sabin right now, he'd

throttle the man. He'd teach him a lesson he would never forget.

But then, he realized suddenly, if Russ had responded as a real man ought to have, nurturing and protecting the woman he'd sworn to love for better or for worse, Jess wouldn't be here now with Nate.

There was a part of him that was selfishly thankful Russ had turned Jess away, though he felt guilty for having such feelings.

If Jess was his wife, he would cherish and protect her with his last breath. It was the same flare of masculine emotion he felt for Gracie; yet at the same time, what he felt for Jess was completely different.

At that moment, Gracie wailed, kicking at Nate's back with her amazingly strong little legs and fisting her hands into his hair.

"Ow!" he exclaimed when she gave an exceptionally hard yank. "Take it easy, little one."

He reached behind him to untangle the baby's fingers, wondering how she had gotten such a firm grip in his inch-long hair. It must really be getting shaggy.

"Okay, sweetheart. That's enough of that, thank you very much."

To Nate's surprise—and relief—Jess laughed. "I think she's trying to tell you she's tired of being in the backpack."

"Or maybe that I need a haircut," he suggested with a grin, shuffling the backpack off his shoulders. Jess leaned in to help shuck it off, and soon baby Gracie was wiggling on Jess's lap.

He didn't consciously decide to slide his arm around her shoulders. It was as natural a move as the breath he took, and completely in line with the cacophony of his feelings for her.

"I don't know how you did it. I don't think I could have. And then you went to work as a day care director," he mused softly, running a palm over the baby's soft, smooth curls.

"Not that you aren't the best at what you do," he hastened to add, squeezing her shoulder. "But I'd imagine that would have been hard for you to work with children, given the circumstances."

"It was. And it wasn't. I've been working in day care since I graduated from college, and there was nothing else I've ever wanted to do, career-wise."

She paused, her gaze distant. "It was tough to go back. I have my good moments and my bad moments, but all in all, it's been kind of therapeutic for me to continue working with children. It's my passion and my ministry. I can't really imagine doing anything else with my life. And Morningway Lodge has been good to me. I've found peace here."

"I'm thankful you were here when I arrived," Nate said earnestly. "I know I would have been at a complete loss with Gracie if you hadn't been here to help us."

Jess nodded and kissed Gracie's forehead, laughing when the baby squirmed in protest. "Gracie is extraspecial. In many ways she reminds me of Elizabeth, but always in a good way. Maybe that's why I feel so unusually attached to her, as I have from the very first moment I laid my eyes on her that first day you came to the lodge."

Nate could see the strain on her face as she spoke. None of this had been easy on her, and he realized he had inadvertently bounded into her life and played a part in causing her pain.

"I'm sorry," he said aloud.

Jess smiled tenuously. "So am I. But God was faithful even when people weren't. When I was in the blackest part of my grief, God reached out to me and pulled me through it, put me back on my feet again. Don't get me wrong. I still struggle. I still worry." Her eyes took on a luminous quality as they met his gaze and held.

A burning lump of emotion lodged in Nate's throat and, for a moment, he could not speak. He stared at her, his heart full of longing.

"You really believe that, don't you? In spite of everything you've been through, your faith in God is strong."

He couldn't relate. He'd persistently turned away from God, using every bad thing that happened in his life, every worldly tragedy he saw, as an excuse to go his own way. And yet the sum total of all of that was nothing in comparison to the personal agony Jess had gone through.

Jess shook her head. "No, that's not quite right, I don't think."

"What?"

"Not *in spite* of everything I've been through. *Because* of what I've been through, my faith is strong," she amended thoughtfully. "But it wasn't until I looked back on my life that I could see how God had carried me through the dark times, even when I cast the blame for my circumstances squarely at His feet. It's a long road. It took me a long time to accept that God loved me unconditionally, no strings attached, but when I finally did, He gave me the courage to go on."

Nate envied her that courage. He had faced IEDs threatening to blow up in his face with less fear than he had about facing his Maker.

He shook his head. "I don't know, Jess. You're a stronger person than me."

Her gaze widened. "Why, Nathan Morningway, I think that is the most foolish thing I've ever heard come out of your mouth," she teased.

"Well, it's true."

"No, Nate. It isn't," she replied softly. "All of us are weak. It's only when we realize our limitations that God can reach us with His strength."

Nate felt a sense of panic surge through him and he didn't know why.

She reached out a hand and laid it on his forearm. "Stop running," she encouraged him. "In our weakness, He is made strong."

Chapter Thirteen

Jessica didn't know what to expect after she and Nate talked, so she was more than a little surprised when Nate showed up bright and early Sunday morning, offering her a ride to church.

Relieved and surprised.

She'd never known a man like Nate Morningway. Even yesterday, as the words had burst out of her mouth that wiped her past clean, she knew Nate would never judge her for it.

She trusted him. She cared for him. And heaven help her, she was starting to see a future with him and that darling baby girl he now called his own.

The notion of offering herself up to any kind of relationship, any form of commitment, still frightened the socks off her.

But Nate himself, not so much.

She felt a lot of things for Nate, but not fear. As she'd learned the hard way, no one was completely faithful and unchanging, except for God. But Nate, she knew, would always do his best not to let her down.

As she would him.

While Nate's presence at church Sunday morning was a surprise in itself, his introspective attitude was even more confounding. Usually boisterous and out-going, Nate had acted peculiarly quiet and thoughtful after the service and all during the drive home.

She'd remembered catching his gaze several times during the service. She thought he looked as if he was wrestling with something inside himself, and by the time they'd reached the car and Nate had yet to say a word, she was sure of it.

She hoped he might reveal to her what it was he was thinking so seriously about, but he continued to be silent, and she didn't ask. He was polite, but dis-tant, and Jessica began to doubt herself and her earlier assurance that everything was working out between them.

What if Nate *couldn't* handle all the information she'd piled on him? What if it was too much?

Over and over she thought about asking him out-right what was bothering him, but she wasn't sure she really wanted to hear the answer.

"Do you want to stay for lunch?" she asked him when he pulled the Jeep up in front of her cabin. "Noth-ing fancy, but I have some cold cuts for sandwiches."

Nate looked at her for a long time, almost as if she had spoken to him in a foreign language and he hadn't understood what she was saying to him.

What's wrong? she wanted to scream.

But of course, she didn't. She just sat frozen in her seat, staring back at him and wringing her hands together in her lap.

She wasn't even consciously aware of her stressed movement, but Nate clearly noticed. He leaned across the seat and laid his large hand over both of hers, stilling them.

"Maybe another time," he said gruffly, and tried to smile.

She thought her own answering grin wasn't any more convincing.

Again, Nate noticed. He brushed the rough pad of his thumb across her cheek, then pushed the corner of her mouth upward.

"It's going to be fine, beautiful Jess," he murmured. "It will all be okay."

Jessica wasn't sure of that. She wasn't even certain to what Nate might be referring. But she shrugged and nodded anyway.

"I know."

He smiled again, this time soft and genuine. "Tomorrow, then?"

She started to nod again, and then cocked her head to one side. "What's tomorrow?"

"You're going with me to tell Vince about the permit." He paused and screwed his lips into a wry pout. "You will go with me to tell Vince about the permit, won't you, honey?"

How could she resist him when he looked at her that way, his golden eyes glowing with warmth?

"Yes," she replied, knowing that was the only answer Nate would accept, and the only answer she wanted to give. "Yes, of course."

Nate couldn't seem to brush off the uneasy feeling that was hovering over him like a little black rain cloud. He tried to tell himself it was just that he had to confront his brother—*again*—with who knew what kind of a result waiting for him.

But that wasn't it.

Ever since Jess had told him the story of her past, he had been haunted by her words.

Because of what I've been through, my faith is strong.

And it was. With all the horrible tragedy the woman had experienced, she was a walking, breathing testament to God's existence and love.

Nate still didn't understand how that could be. He'd thought about it day and night. He'd gone to church and felt like the worst of all hypocrites, his own unbelief pointing its finger at him in accusation.

He'd thought maybe if he gave himself some time, he could sort it all out in his mind. He'd excused himself from having lunch with Jess, knowing she would see right through any kind of façade he hoped to establish. And then he'd spent a restless night tossing and turning, despite the fact that Gracie had peaceably slept the whole night through.

He was no closer to an answer now than he'd been twenty-four hours earlier, though he was a good deal more weary. And Jess was no doubt waiting for him to pick her up this morning so they could go tell Vince the good news about the permit.

Jess. He ought to be focusing on her.

Now that he knew the whole story of her past, he understood the oddity of her hot-and-cold moments. He got why she unconsciously sent him mixed signals.

And he knew, now more than ever, that he wanted—*needed*—to be the man in her future, the one who *didn't* leave her when the going got tough.

Gracie needed her as well—to be the soft, feminine influence every little girl needed in her life. Jess offered Gracie something he never could give.

But Nate knew that in order to have the chance to be those things to Jess, he needed to speak the words that lingered quietly in his heart. It wasn't going to be enough just to show her. She needed to hear the sentiment from his own lips.

As always, he broke into a sweat just thinking about trying to put his emotions into words. What could he say that Jess would believe?

He was still pondering the dilemma when he picked Jess up from her cabin and they dropped Gracie off at the day care center.

Not surprisingly, Jess was acting a little withdrawn this morning. He couldn't blame her. In this instance, he had been the one who'd been sending mixed signals, and he knew it.

"Well, I guess it's now or never," he commented as he pulled the Jeep in front of the main lodge, breaking into the uncomfortable silence that had hovered over them for the entire ride over from the day care.

She stared at him for a moment, then smiled shakily. "Are you ready?"

"As ready as I'll ever be," he replied with a clipped nod. "Let's do it."

Nate took her hand as they entered the lodge and walked up to the guest services counter. He half expected her to pull away, and was glad when she didn't. He needed her support more than she could possibly realize.

He rang the bell on the desk and waited, his muscles tensing as if ready to spring into a quick getaway.

His marine training, he thought. Anticipating disaster was second nature to him now, and from where he stood, he felt as if he was facing a minefield.

The sensation increased when Vince came out of the office, his expression going from polite reserve to anger the moment he saw that it was Nate standing on the other side of the desk.

"What do you want?" Vince snapped without preamble, his brow lowering over his eyes.

"We're here with good news," Jess exclaimed, giving Nate's hand a tug, as if to remind him it was time for him to step up and take control of the conversation.

"Yeah? And what would that be?" Vince asked, crossing his arms over his chest in a combination of a protective and distancing manner.

Nate leaned his forearm on the counter, closing the space between himself and Vince.

"I spent most of the week in Boulder," he began briskly.

To Nate's surprise, Vince's expression turned to that of wary concern. "Where's Gracie? Did something happen? Is she okay?"

"Gracie is fine," Nate assured him. "We dropped her off at the day care before we came up here."

"Oh. I see," said Vince, who visibly relaxed for just a split second before drawing himself back up to his full height. "Then what's the problem?"

"I've been to see the county inspector."

Nate held up his hand when Vince would have interrupted. "I know it may look like I'm messing with your business, Vince, but that's not how it is."

"How is it, then?" Vince asked acerbically, refusing to back down from his hostile stance.

"Look," Nate said, blowing out a breath to steady a surge of anger and doing his best to placate his unreasonable older brother. Getting mad wouldn't help his case any. "This whole building permit fiasco was my fault, so I thought it was only right that I be the one to clear it up."

He dug into his pocket and laid the signed permit in front of Vince. "It's a done deal. You—*we*," he amended when Jess nudged him, "can get that shed built now, before we get socked with a bad winter storm. Oh—and as of right now, the lodge is officially in the 'no fine' zone."

Vince studied the paper for a moment, his expression unreadable. Finally, he looked up, locking his gaze with Nate's.

"We?"

Again, Jess nudged Nate with her elbow.

He *got* it, already.

"Yes, *we*," Nate answered, his gaze flitting to wink at Jess before settling back on Vince. "Two heads are better than one, and all that. I figured since I plan on staying around for a while, I might as well be doing something useful."

Jess gasped and dropped Nate's hand. He turned to find her staring up at him, wide-eyed.

His shrug was meant for both Jess and Vince. "It's no big deal."

But it *was* a big deal, and all three of them knew it. There was a tense moment of silence while each of them were lost in their own thoughts.

Unable to take the strain of the sudden quiet, Nate thrust his right hand forward, toward Vince.

His brother just looked at Nate's extended hand for a

moment without moving. Then, just as Nate was about to pull away, Vince suddenly put his hand forward and shook with Nate.

"Thanks for the permit," Vince said, pocketing the piece of paper.

"And the shed?" Nate prodded. "Do you want my help with it?"

Vince shrugged as if it didn't matter one way or the other, but Nate saw a sparkle of something in Vince's blue eyes that he hadn't seen before.

Acceptance?

"Do what you want, Nate," Vince said. "I'll be out here in the morning to work on the shed. With or without you."

It was as close to a peace offering as Nate knew he was going to get from his bullheaded brother, and he couldn't help but smile—first at Vince, whose frown never wavered, and then at Jess, who beamed back at him, showing without words that she knew he'd just won this battle, and that she was celebrating the victory with him.

Nate turned back to Vince.

"Done," he said, keeping his voice a clipped, businesslike monotone that belied the elation pounding in his chest. "I'll see you tomorrow morning, then."

"Whatever," Vince said grudgingly, and Nate just laughed.

"That went well," Jessica commented shyly. They'd been sitting in the Jeep for five minutes now, and Nate had yet to say a word, much less make any kind of effort to turn the key in the ignition to take them back to the day care to pick up Gracie.

He looked at her as if he was surprised she'd spoken to him.

"It did, didn't it?" he said, bemused. "What do you know?"

"I told you Vince would act rationally once he'd had time to think things over."

Nate flashed her a twisted grin.

"And now that you've solved his problem for him, I would hope that things will be better between the two of you."

"Do you think?" He chuckled. "Don't forget that I was the one who created the problem in the first place. I'm sure Vince won't."

"It's a start," she insisted, patting her knees for emphasis. "A good start."

"I don't know, Jess. I've spent all these years resenting Vince, but lately I've realized that the real problem is with me."

"No, it's not," she denied instantly, then paused thoughtfully. She wasn't doing Nate any kind of favor by blurting out her opinion before she'd listened to what he had to say. "I'm sorry, Nate. Go on."

"I don't know. I'm struggling, but I'm not sure why." He paused, squeezing his fists against the steering wheel. "Can I ask you a question?"

"Of course." She was both curious and hopeful as to what he would say.

"The other day, when you told me about Russ and Elizabeth, you explained how God got you through the bad times."

"Yes, that's true. He carries me through the bad times and rejoices with me in the good. I'm not saying faith in God erased my pain, or made it somehow magically easy for me. It's not. I struggle every day."

"You do?" he asked, sounding genuinely perplexed. "I wouldn't have guessed that. I mean, I know you have your problems, but you seem so joyful."

"I'm only human."

Nate nodded. "I know. It's just that you have such a sense of peace about you. I want that. I've been trying to do the right things with my life, for Gracie's sake as much as my own, but nothing I do seems to help. No matter how hard I try, I just don't perceive the world the way you do, with your faith."

"Maybe you're trying too hard," she suggested softly, reaching out to stroke his biceps.

"What else can I do?"

Jessica looked at Nate for a long moment, seeing him through new eyes. Here was a man who had worked hard for every single thing he had ever received in his life. He was a self-made man in the very best sense of all of those words.

So it just made sense that he would approach God the same way he approached everything else in his life. By putting Gracie ahead of himself. By asking himself what he could *do*. By measuring himself up to some impossible standard he'd created in his own mind.

"I think maybe you're approaching the idea of faith in God all wrong," she suggested tentatively, not wanting to inadvertently hurt his feelings.

"I am? How?"

"Being in a relationship with God isn't what you do. It's who you are."

Nate blanched a sickly white color. "I'm in trouble, then."

Jessica was taken aback. Nate had always exuded self-confidence. It was one of the things she admired most about him. And now he was demeaning himself with surprising fervency.

"Why do you say that?"

He shook his head, a wild look in his eyes, as if he was being pursued by something, as if he was the prey in some crazy hunt.

Jessica squeezed his arm. "What is it? Talk to me, hon."

"You know me better than anyone, Jess. When I should have been turning to God, I shunned Him. And now that I suddenly see how foolish I've been, and how much I want Gracie to grow up in the very faith I despised as a youth, you want me to believe God will just turn a blind eye and accept me the way I am?"

He didn't sound as if he believed it could be possible, and Jessica knew exactly how he felt. The circumstances were different, but at the heart of it all, not too long ago, she had been in the same place, spiritually speaking, that Nate was in now.

"God accepts you for who you are," she explained quietly, praying for the right words to make Nate understand. "But it's not because He blinds himself to your faults. He knows everything, Nate, and He loves you anyway."

He stared at her, unspeaking.

"The Scriptures say that while we were yet sinners, Christ died for us."

His mouth compressed into a tight line and his face became even more grim.

"But how can He…" His question drifted off into silence.

"I know that's a lot to wrap your mind around," she continued. "But it's true."

Nate reached for the ignition and gunned the Jeep into motion. Jessica thought to say more, but she could see she had overwhelmed him with what she'd already said. She drew her hand away from his arm and clasped her hands together in her lap, praying silently for God to reach Nate with His love, the way He had in her heart and life.

As Nate maneuvered down the road, he kept his gaze facing forward. Jessica watched him out of her peripheral vision, noting the stony expression on his face. With the way he was reacting, she maybe ought to have been worried about him, but her soul was oddly at peace.

God was clearly at work in Nate's heart, and she was thankful for both Nate's sake and for baby Gracie's. When all was said and done, Jessica had faith that God would prevail, even with tough, stubborn, single-minded Nathan Morningway.

God had reached her stone-cold heart when she didn't think anyone or anything could. She was so thankful that God was greater than their sins, even stubbornness and disbelief.

There was no doubt about it. Nate might be fighting it, but his heart was softening.

And when that final barrier had been broken, Jessica thought she might just lose her heart to Nate, once and for all.

Chapter Fourteen

Nate's mind was a million miles away as he tried to wrap his thoughts around what Jess had said to him. It all appeared so monumentally complicated in his mind, but Jess made it sound simple and uncomplicated. Somehow she streamlined it in his mind in a way he hadn't thought of before.

What it boiled down to, Nate realized with a start, was faith.

Even after all his time with Jess, faith wasn't an easy concept for Nate to grasp. Yet in a way he could not begin to explain, he *felt* it—God's presence—as the truth of the Scriptures made the slow migration from his head to his heart.

"What is that?" Jess asked, pointing over the ridge in the direction Nate was driving. "Look at all the smoke. Is something burning?"

"Probably just a barrel of trash," he answered, still in a hazy state of mind. Then he glanced to where she was pointing and pressed down hard on the accelerator. The Jeep leaped forward in time with Nate's heart.

This was no burning barrel of trash. The smoke

billowing out over the top of the tree line was too thick and too black to be an organized burn. His gut clenched as he realized he was driving right into it.

The day care.

Gracie was there, along with at least a dozen other small children and two teachers.

"Nate?" Jess questioned uncertainly.

Nate flashed a quick, encouraging glance at her, most of his concentration on maneuvering the Jeep across the washboarded dirt road at the highest speed he dared. He hoped the shock and panic registering on Jess's expression didn't reflect his own gaze.

"The day care!" Jess exclaimed. "Oh, God help us. Nate, hurry!"

Responding to the horror in her tone, Nate gunned the engine, clasping the wheel tightly with both hands as the Jeep fishtailed around a curve. In moments, they had crested the ridge and could see into the valley where the day care was located.

At his first glimpse of the flames and smoke pouring from the burning building, the knifing pain in his belly stabbed into his chest and throat. As he drove nearer, the black, ugly clouds of smoke billowing from the front windows seemed to be blocking out the sunlight. Flames surged from the windows on the east side of the building.

The day care, like all of the other buildings on the Morningway retreat grounds, was built to resemble a rustic, old-fashioned log cabin. Nate wondered, fighting down panic, how fast a structure such as this one would burn to the ground.

Too fast.

Nate took in the whole chaotic scene at once. One

of the teachers was ushering a handful of preschoolers away from the burning building. The children were surprisingly subdued, given the circumstances. They moved in an organized line. The teacher, an older woman, was scurrying back and forth between the front and back of the line, pointing toward the trees and encouraging the children to walk faster, away from the burning structure.

Nate refocused his gaze on the building itself just as the second teacher emerged from the front door, covered with soot. She carried a little girl under her arm like a football and was pulling another child, a little boy, by the hand. Scooping the boy up in her other arm, she rushed toward where the other teacher and the children now stood, hunched in small groups near the tree line.

He heard Jess praying under her breath, her fists clenching the dashboard as she leaned forward to survey the scene. "Lord, help us."

Nate sped into the parking lot and punched on the brake. The Jeep slid several feet on the loose gravel under the tires.

Jess was out the door before the Jeep had slid to a stop.

"Jess, no!" Nate cried out. He reached out to grab her, to stop her from putting herself in harm's way, as he knew instinctively she had every intention of doing. Like him, her only thought was for Gracie and the other children trapped in the inferno.

His hand met empty air. Jess was already rushing toward the burning building.

Nate looked after her for a split second that felt like a lifetime, his entire being supplicating God for help as Jess disappeared through the billow of black smoke coming through the open front door of the building. His stomach lurched and he swallowed hard, forcing down the increasing sense of fear and panic eroding his thoughts.

Focus, he ordered himself, forcing a breath into lungs that appeared to have stopped working.

He jammed his hand into the front pocket of his bomber jacket and retrieved his cell phone, while with the other hand he was putting the Jeep into Park and shutting down the ignition.

His first instinct was to run in after Jess, but he wasn't sure if either of the teachers now huddling over the children near the tree line had a cell phone with them, nor if they would have the presence of mind to make the necessary call.

It looked as if they had all they could do just to contain the gaggle of children, some of whom were staring wide-eyed at the blaze, others who were chattering up at the adults, though Nate could barely hear them through the ringing in his own ears. He felt a little dizzy, and he realized he was hyperventilating.

He had to pull it together, to remain in control, for Jess's sake now as well as Gracie's. His military training finally kicked in, slowing his pulse and his breathing so he could think.

He jumped down from the Jeep and was racing toward the front of the day care center even as he punched in the emergency number. Thankfully, a new cell tower had recently been built just north of the Morningway property, and the signal on his phone was strong. After just one ring, the emergency dispatcher picked up.

"911. What is the nature of your emergency?"

"This is Nathan Morningway of Morningway Lodge," he said, enunciating every word. "We need the fire department here right away. The day care center is on fire. I think there are still some little kids inside. I don't know how many."

One, for sure. His baby.

His baby!

He paused before the entrance of the building and gave the emergency dispatcher all the necessary information on the location. Fear like he'd never experienced before clutched at his chest, and he could barely think past the pain.

What if he lost Gracie—or Jess?

No!

He couldn't—wouldn't—think that way. He had to get into that building and get them out of there.

Alive.

"Please stay on the line, sir," the dispatcher said in the calm, determined manner to which Nate knew she had been trained.

"Just get them here quickly," Nate replied. "I've got to go. My daughter is in there."

Panic preceded every thought as he snapped the phone closed and took one last deep breath before plunging into the smoky room, ducking as low as he could to the floor while still at a dead run, one arm sheltering his mouth and nose.

He couldn't see a thing through the black smoke, so he reached out his other arm in front of him, hoping to feel his way around, if it came to that.

Suddenly he felt a hand on his arm.

It was Jess. He could barely see her through the

haze and the way the smoke stung his eyes, but she was there, holding a handkerchief over her mouth and nose and gesturing with her free hand, pointing back toward the front door where he'd just entered.

What was she trying to tell him?

Jessica's hand slid from Nate's upper arm and clasped to his wrist in an iron grip. She tugged in earnest, but he was so tense his arm didn't budge. She knew he couldn't see anything through the thick smoke, and the fire was roaring too loudly for him to hear her speak. Touch was her only choice in finding a means to communicate with him.

She fought down the rising surge of panic. They were running out of time, and she couldn't get Nate to move in the right direction.

She yanked harder and felt him subtly shift. Desperate for him to understand, she dragged his hand in front of her, waist-high, where several children were huddled. When his fingers connected with one young boy's silky hair, she felt him freeze as the realization of what she wanted finally hit him.

When she'd burst into the building moments earlier, she'd found five small preschoolers huddling under the art table. Her first thought had been to go for Gracie, but she couldn't abandon these tiny innocents to the elements, no matter how much her heart cried out for the baby she knew was in the next room.

The children had been terrified and afraid to move, and she hadn't been able to reassure them with her voice. Dropping to her knees, she'd gathered them in front of her, in her arms, and then was attempting to push and prod them toward the door and safety when Nate had materialized next to her.

They needed to get these kids out, so they could get to Gracie before it was too late. The raging fire itself wasn't the only danger. Jessica was already feeling the effects of smoke inhalation despite the handkerchief over her nose and mouth. Granted, the children were smaller and therefore lower to the ground, but the thick, merciless smoke had to be affecting them, as well.

And Gracie…

Panic surged again, painful in its intensity, but she tamped it back, willing herself to focus and concentrate on what needed to be done.

Nate nodded frantically, letting Jessica know he understood what she was trying to tell him. She let go of his wrist, and a moment later, he had a mopheaded little girl in one arm and a young boy in the other. Jerking his head in the direction, he turned, he lurched toward the front door.

Jessica was right on his heels, holding one toddler in her arms and clasping the other two by the hands, dragging them forward with a momentum she hardly believed she possessed, fear and adrenaline making up for whatever strength she might have lacked.

They all burst outside at the same time. The sunshine temporarily blinded her as she choked and coughed and propelled the children forward, toward the teachers and the rest of the waiting children.

"How many?" she choked out, aiming her question no one teacher in particular.

"Thirteen," called Miss Cathy, who was in charge when Jessica wasn't present. The sheer panic on her face, along with the older woman huddled over the children at the tree line, matched the turmoil in Jessica's own heart.

"We've got them all, Jessica, except for Gracie," Miss Cathy continued hastily. "I'm sorry. The chaos. I couldn't leave the children to—"

"Keep those children away from the building," Nate ordered, sternly staring down first one teacher, then the other, looking ominous and almost threatening with swirls of ash lining his powerful face.

He whirled and ran full-force back toward the building. Jessica was right on his heels. After a moment, he became aware she was following him and tossed a stern glare over his shoulder.

"Go back with the children," he barked in the same no-nonsense voice that had worked so well with the teachers and, Jessica imagined, dozens of marines over his years in the service.

"No way," she uttered through gritted teeth.

She was determined to continue back into the building, no matter what Nate thought, and she only balked for a moment at his harsh tone before starting forward again, resolve in every step, moving at such a quick pace she soon rushed in front of him.

"Jess," he roared, reaching out to grab her arm in a viselike grip. "Go back. I don't have time to argue with you."

"Then don't. We have to get Gracie!" Panic edged her voice, but her movements were surprisingly firm.

"I'll get Gracie," he said, pulling her backward and stepping in front of her. "You go back. The children need you."

"Gracie needs me," she insisted, jerking her arm away from his grip and dashing into the day care, gagging as the smoke pierced her lungs, thicker even than it had been before. She ducked down, trying to avoid the worst of the smoke.

Nate burst through the door moments after Jessica, ducking down just as Jessica had, and gestured for her to go ahead of him. She knew the way better than he did, and she was glad he was no longer fighting for her to leave the scene.

She moved without hesitation into the adjoining area, the nursery, and immediately moved to the left side of the room. Cribs ran the circumference of the room, and she frantically struggled to get her bearings for what felt like hours but was probably only seconds.

The smoke was so thick she hardly knew which way was up. She prayed as she hastened toward what she hoped was the crib where she usually placed Gracie when she was working in the day care, hoping that the other teachers had placed her in the same spot.

A beam right above their heads cracked ominously, and Jessica ducked instinctively, then staggered the last few feet to the crib. She couldn't see him, but she sensed Nate was right behind her.

Her eyes and her lungs burned with the effort, but as she approached, she thought she saw movement from within the crib, though with the thick smoke, she couldn't be certain.

Panic surged through her once again.

Gracie!

She had to get to the baby.

Without another thought, she reached for the metal latch that would release the side of the crib.

"Jess, no!" he tried to scream, but the heavy smoke billowed into his lungs and he gagged instead.

His warning, even if he'd been able to voice it, had come too late. Jess wrapped her bare hand around the metal latch and then jolted and staggered backward, cradling her burned skin close to her chest. Her mouth was open, but no sound emerged.

She would have fallen, but Nate darted forward and swept her against him, one arm wrapped firmly around her waist and the other urging her mouth closed.

More than one beam cracked and whined above them, and the heat was growing more intense by the second. He was feeling woozy again, but he fought the sensation with every fiber of his being.

As from a great distance, he heard the sound of sirens, but he knew he didn't have time to wait for the firefighters to help with the rescue. He had to get his baby girl and the woman he loved out of this building before the whole thing came down on them.

Pulling Jess with him, he reached over the edge of the crib, relief flooding through him when his hand made contact with the baby's head. Gracie was sitting up, her arms flapping in distress.

Nate reached for her, but Jess was faster.

Ignoring her own injury, Jess plucked Gracie from the crib and tucked her as far beneath her jacket as the material would allow, trying to protect the baby from additional smoke inhalation. The action left Jess's own lungs unprotected from the smoke, and put her at the very great risk of losing consciousness.

He had to get them out *now*.

He reached out and grabbed the collar of Jess's coat, dragging her with him to the nearest window. His head was swimming from the lack of oxygen, but his mind was amazingly focused on this single task.

Get them out alive.

There was no time to work their way back to the front door, and Nate suspected the fire had made the route impassable, in any case.

Sending up a silent prayer for his actions to work, he turned sideways to the window, bent his elbow and slammed into the glass.

Pain shot through his shoulder as the glass splintered but did not break. Knowing there was no time to waste, he ignored the pain, gritted his teeth and threw his shoulder into the window again.

This time, the glass shattered under the full force of his weight. Nate gasped as oxygen poured through the window, but his relief was short-lived as the fire all around them flared to a new intensity, being fed by the burst of air.

The blaze was growing worse by the second, and Nate didn't hesitate as he pulled the sleeve of his bomber jacket over his right hand and thrust his arm around all four sides of the windowpane, jarring loose jagged edges of glass so the three of them could crawl through to safety.

Two firefighters, dressed in full regalia and face masks, reached for Nate's arms, gesturing for him to crawl through the window.

Nate balked and jerked away from their grasp. He wasn't about to go through that window until Jess and Gracie were safe.

Jess nudged Nate's side with her shoulder, then shoved the now-limp baby into his arms, gesturing wildly toward the window.

Nate wanted Jess to exit with Gracie, but he knew she wouldn't budge until the baby was safe.

He stepped forward, ⌐   :cie at the two firefighters. The baby had clearly lost consciousness, and terror such as Nate had never known coursed through him. He prayed with all his might that they had not arrived too late to save her.

If he lost Gracie…

No.

He couldn't think of that now. Jess was still standing behind him, and she was still in very great danger from the flames around them.

He spun on his heels and reached his arms to her, intending to catapult her through the window and into the waiting arms of the firefighters.

But this nightmare was far from over. He didn't even know for sure that they hadn't missed any little children when they had evacuated the building. He prayed the teacher's head count had been right.

He could only react to the moment and pray for the best.

Only seconds had passed, but it felt like hours. He stepped toward Jess, his arms outstretched. Jess reached back to him.

Their fingers met. Their eyes met through the smoky haze. Fear masked her face, but Nate read determination there, as well. He would have sighed in relief if he could have breathed at all.

Most people, Nate thought, would have let fear take advantage of them, freezing them immobile.

But not Jess.

Not his Jess.

They both heard the hiss and crack of the beam directly overhead before they saw it. As if in slow motion, Jess looked up, and Nate followed her gaze.

Sparks rained down on them, the only warning they had before the beam came loose and pitched downward.

Jess let go of Nate's hand and instinctively sheltered her head, but it was too late.

The heavy beam of flaming wood crashed down on top of her. She jerked, her eyes wide in surprise, and reached out for Nate. Then she fell lifeless as the beam slammed into her shoulder and crushed her beneath its weight.

"Jess!" Nate screamed, scrambling forward. He fell to his knees as a wave of dizziness overtook him, but he continued to crawl forward, fighting the looming blackness with all his might.

A dry sob wracked his body as he reached Jess's unmoving form, covered horizontally by the fallen beam of wood.

He wanted to cry.

He wanted to pray.

But one thought obscured all the rest. He didn't know nor did he care whether it was just in his head, or whether he was screaming out loud.

This couldn't be happening.

Not Jess. Not Jess. Not Jess.

"No-o-o-o-o!"

Chapter Fifteen

Nate lunged forward, his arms outstretched toward Jess, and then slammed to his hands and knees on the floor when his forward momentum was crushed by someone suddenly clasping his ankle in a firm grip.

Groaning, he glanced behind him. The two firemen who had been at the window had now entered the building. The first one, clutching Nate's ankle in a viselike grip, was now pulling him backward. The second firefighter was gesturing at Nate and pointing toward the broken window and their only means of escape.

Nate's gaze swung back to Jess. She wasn't moving. He couldn't tell if she was breathing.

He knew what the firefighters wanted him to do.

Exit. Immediately.

Leave the rescuing to the experts, the men who were well-versed in what flames and smoke could do.

They might be heroes. And they might be right. Nate could hinder them as much as he could help them, especially if they became more focused on getting him out alive than in rescuing Jess.

His heart and his mind tugged in two different directions, but only for a split second. He relaxed his leg for a moment and then yanked hard, surprising the man who was gripping his ankle and breaking away.

He scrambled forward, his heart slamming into his chest. His lungs felt as if they were going to explode, but he ignored the sensation and plunged ahead through the billowing smoke.

He was thankful his mind was military-hardwired for crisis, for otherwise he never would have been able to keep it together.

Kneeling beside Jess, he leaned forward, checking her vital signs and praying all the while.

She wasn't moving.

But she was breathing. Barely.

And that beam had to weigh a ton. It was crushing her. Thankfully, it didn't appear to be burning, though it was no doubt smoldering.

He scrambled to the side, where the end of the beam lay at an upward angle, jutting off Jess's back. He had to get that rafter off her *now*. Then he could figure out how to move her without harming her more than she already probably was.

It looked bad.

He felt worse.

He didn't know what was sensible anymore. He only knew he had to do something, and pray it was the right thing. Pulling his jacket sleeves over his hands for protection, he wrapped his arms around the rafter and pulled with all his might.

Nothing.

The beam didn't so much as budge.

Nate couldn't see if there was anything covering

the other end of the rafter, but he thought it might be lodged tight in some other debris. A lot had fallen from the ceiling when the beam gave way.

He wished he could see better.

He wished he could breath at all.

He had to move that beam.

Praying with all his might, he embraced the adrenaline coursing through him and felt his fear. He knew from experience his terror would either render him useless or give him extra strength.

The first firefighter reached Jess and was assessing her condition. The other man had gone back toward the window. Nate didn't know why he was backtracking, nor did he care.

He closed his eyes, gritted his teeth and pulled, straining every muscle in his back and shoulders and legs. Sweat streamed into his eyes, stinging them with the ash covering his forehead. He coughed and gagged from the smoke and the exertion.

But the rafter moved.

Nate didn't hesitate for an instant. Bracing himself, he leaned into it, forcing the wood away from Jess's upper body and hoping the momentum created by his weight and his effort would be enough to make the rafter clear her legs and feet.

The beam came crashing down to the floor again, splintering bits of wood and plaster underneath it, and Nate winced. If he hadn't moved it far enough, he had just added to Jess's injuries.

The same firefighter that had grabbed his ankle earlier suddenly appeared at his elbow, thumping him on the shoulder and urging him back toward the window. Ignoring him, Nate dropped to his hands and knees and scuttled forward, desperate to see if he had, in fact, pushed the rafter far enough to clear Jess's body, or if he'd merely pinned her anew.

It was difficult to see anything through the thick, black smoke, but his hand made contact with Jess's foot. The smoldering beam lay several inches past the end of her body.

She was free.

But not yet safe.

The firefighter he had repeatedly brushed off was at his elbow again, this time grasping Nate firmly by the shoulders and propelling him toward the window, brooking no argument.

This time Nate didn't fight back, but allowed himself to be pushed wherever the fireman willed. His lungs were screaming for oxygen. He wasn't going to be any help to anyone if he passed out, especially if he was still within the building.

It was time to let the firefighters do their jobs, he thought, his whole body suddenly so weak he could barely move. As he crawled through the broken window, he could see they had already placed a collar around Jess's neck and were rolling her onto a board.

Nate fell to his knees when he hit the ground on the outside of the building. Smoke and flames billowed through the window he'd just dropped from, but close to the ground, he was able to take great, sweeping breaths of outside air, which sent him into a fit of coughing that wracked his aching body.

He had to move.

For Jess. For Gracie.

But he found he couldn't. His arms and legs felt

impossibly heavy, and his mind was clogged and dizzy, almost as if he had been drugged. A persistent, angry headache was slamming at his temples.

He had nothing left to give, he thought miserably. No more strength left to fight with.

And he knew why. He had done everything he could, but his girls might not make it. Grief washed over him in unceasing waves. How would he go on if he lost Jess or Gracie?

Faith.

This was where the rubber met the road. He'd been wrestling with his faith in God. Now was the time to use it.

He reached deep down inside himself, searching for strength, but found none.

And then his soul stretched upward, seeking God's presence as never before.

To his very great surprise, he found it. Or rather, God found him. Strength, peace and love as Nate had never before experienced replaced his fear and set aside his panic. Though his headache persisted, his mind cleared. And though he continued to hack and cough, his soul breathed the fresh air of God's presence.

He groaned and tried to roll to his feet, but he was so shaky he couldn't make it off his hands and knees. He knew he was in the way. Firefighters were pouring out the window, leveraging the board which carried an unconscious Jess. Efficiently and quickly, they passed her through to safety, and the last firefighter crawled through the window after her.

The two paramedics on the scene were already there, rushing to Jess's side as they jogged her farther away from the building. Someone placed an oxygen mask over her face. Nate couldn't see anything else, couldn't tell if she was all right, if anything was broken. Even if he could have seen her, he had no way of knowing if she was going to survive.

Suddenly someone dropped a thick wool blanket over Nate's shoulders. Strong arms looped under his shoulders and drew him to his feet.

Hazily, Nate glanced upward.

Vince.

"Come on now, little brother," Vince said. "You're in the way, as usual."

Vince's teasing tone overlaid his more serious expression. Nate didn't know why Vince was here, but he'd never been as glad to see his brother as he was at that moment.

With Vince's assistance, Nate managed to swerve drunkenly toward the waiting ambulance, where they were already bundling Jess inside.

Behind him there was a big whoosh as the once-solid structure of the day care collapsed from the heat. Firefighters were dousing it with water, but it was far too late to save the building.

But not, Nate prayed, the human beings.

"Gracie," he choked out raggedly, his voice hoarse from the ash he had inhaled. The children huddling by the tree line were being herded into the day care van by the teachers, presumably on their way to be checked out at the hospital in Boulder.

But Nate could see no sign of Gracie.

"Where's my baby?" he rasped, grasping desperately for the collar of Vince's jacket.

"She's already on her way to the hospital," Vince informed him tightly, pulling on his sleeve and urging him to sit down by the ambulance. Nate's knees were shaky and he thought he might fall down if he didn't sit down, so he slumped to the ground.

"How is she? Is she…?" He couldn't seem to get the words out.

Vince crouched in front of Nate and clasped him on the shoulders. "Gracie is already on her way to the hospital in Boulder," he repeated. "The first ambulance took off with her several minutes ago."

A female paramedic approached and Vince stepped away as she placed a pulse-ox monitor on Nate's finger and checked his lungs with her stethoscope. Nate wanted to brush her away, but he was too fatigued to move.

"Is she…?" Nate repeated, unable to complete his thought.

"She's going to be fine," Vince said with a clipped nod. Nate wasn't so sure, from the way his brother set his jaw after he spoke.

"She was unconscious when I passed her through the window."

"I know," Vince said. "But she quickly regained consciousness after the paramedics worked on her and gave her some oxygen."

"Thank God," Nate murmured.

"Amen," Vince answered, sounding as choked up as Nate felt. He chuckled, a dry, forced sound. "It looked to me like Gracie was giving the paramedics a hard time when they bundled her into the ambulance. I think she wanted her daddy."

Nate tried to smile but couldn't.

"I've got to get there," he mumbled, as much to himself as to Nate.

"You will, brother. If I have any say in the matter, you'll be taking this ambulance with Jess."

Nate grimaced. He didn't need medical attention. Jess did. She had been so brave, not thinking of herself at all as she had burst into the blazing building. Were it not for her, there would be many grieving parents right now. Nate most of all.

"And the other kids?" he asked.

"All safe," Vince assured him. "The teachers have contacted all the parents, and they will be using the day care van to take them down to the emergency room to be checked out for smoke inhalation. But the important part is that everyone made it out alive, thanks in great part to you and Jess."

"Jess," Nate repeated, his throat stinging as he spoke, as much from raw emotion as from the smoke he had inhaled.

The female paramedic broke in to tell Nate he could ride along with Jess in the ambulance, but that they needed to go now.

"You're a hero, little brother," Vince said, supporting Nate as he rose. "Foolish, but a hero nonetheless. You saved Jess's life back there."

Nate shook his head, then ducked into the ambulance to take a seat by Jess's still form. He reached out and gently traced her forehead with his finger. He couldn't stand to see her this way, so utterly still and silent and devoid of life.

But she *was* alive, Nate reminded himself. Her chest was rising and falling with precious oxygen, and the paramedics were busy making her stable.

"I'll follow the ambulance down and meet you at

the hospital," Vince told him as the paramedics made to close the doors to the rescue vehicle.

"But the day care—"

"Is a goner. There's nothing I can do here. The fire department has it under control. People before buildings, you know?"

Nate's eyes were stinging again, and he didn't think it was because of the smoke and ash. He swallowed the lump in his throat with difficulty.

"Thank you," he whispered raggedly.

Vince gave a clipped nod and his jaw tightened. "Just be well, Nate. You have a couple of very important ladies depending on you."

Not that Nate needed to be reminded of that very sobering thought, but he thrust out his hand toward Vince anyway. Vince clasped his hand forcefully, and Nate saw that his were not the only eyes watering.

For possibly the first time in his life, he knew what it felt like to have the support of family, Nate thought as the doors closed and the vehicle jerked into motion. He knew Jess would see it as a blessing rising from the ashes of tragedy and she wouldn't have hesitated a moment to tell him so.

And despite the fact that this ordeal was far from over, Nate found to his surprise that he could see the blessing through the tragedy, as well.

Nate wanted to smile, but simultaneously experienced the desire to weep. It wasn't over yet.

Vince thumped Nate on the back. Hard. "Don't scare me like that again, little brother."

"What?" Nate had been gazing down at Gracie, sleeping in a tented bassinet in the hospital neonatal intensive care unit, and his mind had been a million miles away, remembering the moment he had scribbled his signature on the papers that officially proclaimed him the baby girl's legal guardian.

Gracie had turned his life upside down, changed his whole reason for living. Raising a baby was the hardest thing he'd ever done, but it was also the most satisfying. He'd never imagined that the little lady could steal his heart away as she had.

And he'd never imagined he would also find the woman of his dreams. He'd figured his life was pretty much in a holding pattern once he'd become Gracie's guardian. Instead, he'd found Jess.

"What a little darlin'," Vince murmured, keeping one hand on Nate's back as they both leaned over the tented bassinet. "How's she doing?"

Nate breathed out on a sigh. "She's going to be fine. The doctors want to keep her overnight for observation, but they said that if all goes well, I can take her home in the morning."

Vince squeezed Nate's shoulder. "I'm glad. God is good."

"Yes," Nate whispered raggedly.

"And Jessica? Have you heard anything about her condition?"

Nate shook his head. "Not yet. They whisked her away the moment we reached the hospital. I won't be able to see her until they admit her into a room."

"Intensive care?" Vince queried quietly and sympathetically.

He shrugged. "I don't know yet."

"Well, she's not alone. And neither are you. I'll wait with you."

"You don't have to do that. I know you must be anxious to get back to the lodge."

Vince scowled, reminiscent of old times. "You know better than to tell me what to do. I said I'm going to wait with you, and that's exactly what I intend to do. End of subject."

True to his word, Vince stayed by Nate's side as they waited for word on Jess in the emergency waiting room. Nate asked to see her, but as the doctors were working on her, he was not allowed to go in.

All he could think of was how she was alone, how he didn't want her to regain consciousness without him being by her side. If—*when* she opened her eyes, he wanted her to see him there. She had been through enough pain and abandonment in her life. Nate wanted to make sure that didn't happen again.

Ever.

He wished for the hundredth time that day that he had spoken to her earlier, told her the deepest feelings of his heart before it might be too late to tell her at all. There was so much he wanted to say, so much he needed her to know about him. About her.

About them.

But of course he couldn't have said anything to her even if he'd gotten up the nerve, for a very simple reason.

Because he wasn't right with God. And until that happened, it wouldn't be right to ask Jess for more than friendship. She deserved to have a man by her side who shared her precious faith, and Nate wasn't yet that man, though he wanted to be.

For Jess. For Gracie.

But most of all, for himself. He recognized the truth,

and prayed that it would, as the Scriptures said, set him free.

A feeling Nate couldn't begin to explain washed over him as he realized God was no longer on some high, unattainable mountaintop.

The truth *had* set him free.

And it had happened when he had least expected it, in that moment where everything had changed. He had faced his worst nightmare—losing the two people who meant the most in the world to him.

And God had been there.

Nate didn't know what had changed, or why. Only that somehow, the faith he couldn't seem to wrap his mind around had wrapped itself around his heart. It was a mystery he wasn't sure he would ever understand, but he would thank God for it every day of his life.

He couldn't wait to tell Jess the good news. She would be overjoyed at Nate's newfound faith.

If he ever got to tell her.

He was as frightened as he had ever been in his life. He'd already known he'd fallen hard for Jess, but it wasn't until he'd heard the ominous cracking of the beam over her head at the day care that he had realized the true depth and breadth of his love for her.

Somehow he had to convince her his love was real, a forever love that would carry them through the rest of their lives.

He had to tell her.

It had been two hours, and Nate hadn't heard a word. Vince still sat beside him, his head bowed and his hands clasped. Nate thought he might be praying. There was a lot about his brother that Nate didn't know.

Suddenly Nate couldn't sit still a moment longer. He stood and stretched his sore muscles, then tensed as one of the emergency room doctors strode through the double doors that led back to the emergency triage.

The doctor's scrubs looked as wrinkled as his brow. As he glanced expectantly around the waiting room, Nate strode forward.

"I'm looking for information on Jessica Sabin," he said without preamble. "Do you know anything?"

The doctor stared at Nate a moment without answering, and then nodded, his expression serious. "Are you family, sir?"

"I came in on the ambulance with her," Nate said. "She has no family."

Except for me and Gracie, he thought, his chest clenching. "Is she okay?"

The doctor hesitated as if trying to decide whether or not to disclose any information to Nate. Nate drew himself to his full height and took a step forward, grasping the doctor on his upper arm.

"Please. If you know anything...I've been waiting for hours."

Finally, the green-scrubbed doctor nodded. "She is in stable condition. Miraculously, no bones were broken, but she inhaled a lot of smoke. That is our greatest concern at the moment."

"Can I talk to her?"

"I'm sorry, but no. She hasn't yet regained consciousness."

"What?" Nate's grip tightened reflexively on the doctor's arm. Murmuring an apology, Nate took a step back and released his hold on the doctor. "That's bad, isn't it?"

The doctor's lips drew together in a firm line. "It could be."

Nate felt as if he'd been struck as his breath heaved out of his lungs. The roaring in his head intensified and all the colors of the room faded to black and white, like a television with a malfunctioning picture tube.

His knees might have given way, but suddenly Vince was there beside him, propping him up with a strong, steady arm under his.

"Take it easy, there, bro," Vince whispered, loud enough for Nate's ears alone. "Be strong."

Vince turned his attention to the doctor. "So what's the next step? Is there anything you can do to help Jessica regain consciousness?"

The doctor shook his head. "We wait."

Nate pulled back his shoulders and fought against the deafening noise in his head. "Can I see her, please? I just want to be by her side."

"We're moving her upstairs now. Room 455. You can visit her there. What is your name, sir? I'll let the nurses know you'll be coming."

"Nathan Morningway," he answered, a new wave of strength suddenly encompassing him.

Jess would wake up. She had to. And when she did, he would be there.

Chapter Sixteen

Jessica's nose itched.

Without opening her eyes, she reached up to scratch it, but her hand felt unusually heavy, too weighty to lift. There was something lying across her cheekbones, plastic tubing of some kind, she thought drowsily.

How long had she been sleeping?

The air streaming from the tubing was what was making Jessica's nose itch so bad, she realized. She now recognized it must be oxygen tubing draped around her ears, but she couldn't immediately remember where she was or why she needed oxygen.

She tried her left hand and made contact with her nose, but the movement caused the back of her hand to prick with a sharp, needlelike sensation, and her whole body ached as if she had been on the losing end of a fistfight.

Groaning inwardly, she tried to open her eyes.

Where was she?

Light was streaming in through the half-open blinds on the window, and it took a moment for her eyesight to adjust to the brightness. She didn't recognize the room at all, though she now realized the stinging sensation on her left hand was from an IV drip, and her right hand was tightly bandaged.

And she hurt, worse than she ever thought possible. It wasn't localized pain, but more of a radiating muscle ache, everywhere at once.

Panic edged through her as her whereabouts finally struck home. It all came rushing back to her—the fire at the day care. The sting of the black, billowing smoke filling her lungs.

The children. Gracie.

She caught her breath, remembering Nate passing the baby through the window he had smashed out with his elbow, into the arms of the firefighters hovering on the other side.

Gracie was safe. Wasn't she?

What had happened then? The last thing she remembered was hearing the beam above her head hiss and crack, just before it crashed down on her.

She was in a hospital.

She was in pain.

But, she recognized suddenly as her head drifted to the right, she wasn't alone.

There was a reason she hadn't been able to move her right arm up to her face, and it wasn't just that her hand was bandaged.

Nate was here.

He was asleep, slumped in a very uncomfortable-looking chair which he had pulled by her bedside. His head rested at an awkward angle on one of his palms. His other hand gently covered her right shoulder.

Though her muscles ached with the effort, she drew herself carefully to her side. Nate didn't budge. She didn't know how long he'd been sleeping that way, but there was no way he could be comfortable. He must be truly exhausted to be sleeping so soundly in such an awkward position.

Easing her left hand over her body, she reached out and ran her fingers down Nate's stubbly jaw. His chiseled features were boyish and relaxed in sleep, and his hair had grown out enough that it was adorably disheveled and sticking at various angles from his scalp like a ruffled porcupine.

She loved this man. So much so that her heart ached worse than her bruised body.

The thought came so quickly she couldn't have quelled it if she tried—and she didn't even want to try. There was no way to deny the way her heart sang when she was around Nate.

She hadn't been looking for love, but Nate and Gracie had found her anyway. The moment the gruff marine had walked into the doorway of Morningway Lodge toting his sweet baby girl, her life had changed irrevocably.

And, she thought, smiling softly, definitely for the better.

She had been so paralyzed by her past that she couldn't see the good gifts God had given her right under her nose. How could she ever have denied the feelings that were now so prominent in her heart?

Nate gave a cute little snort and jerked awake, his eyes wide as they focused down on her.

"You're awake," he breathed, his voice laced with relief and thankfulness. "Thank God. Jess, you had me so scared."

Jessica tried to nod, but the small movement sent

ripples of pain throbbing through her head and all the way down to her toes. Groaning from deep within her chest, she rolled onto her back.

"Don't try to move, sweetheart. You've been through the ringer. How are you feeling?"

"Gracie?" she croaked through parched lips, ignoring Nate's fervent question about her own health.

Nate smiled and gently brushed her hair off her forehead with his palm. "Gracie is fine, honey. Thanks to you."

She breathed a sigh of relief. "And the rest of the children?"

"Also fine," he confirmed. "Everyone got out of the building safely. In fact, no one else besides you and Gracie had to be hospitalized."

"Hospitalized?" Jessica repeated, horror returning with reinforcements. "I thought you said Gracie was okay?"

Before Nate could answer her harried question, a nurse entered the room.

"I'm glad to see you're awake," the nurse said, hovering over Jessica and wrapping a blood pressure cuff around the upper part of her right arm. She tossed a sideways glance at Nate. "I'll have to ask you to leave now while the doctor checks her out."

"Yes, of course," Nate answered, scooting out of his chair and kissing Jessica on the brow. "I'll be back soon, sweetheart."

"But—" Jessica started, and was interrupted by Nate shaking his head.

"You take it easy." He exited the room with such swiftness that Jessica could not even finish her statement before he was gone.

"And how are we feeling this morning?" the nurse asked compassionately as she jotted the numbers from the blood pressure monitor onto a clipboard.

Jessica licked her dry lips before answering. Her throat was raw and burning.

"Sore," she murmured, punctuated by a low groan as muscles she didn't know she had clenched and released, spasming painfully.

The nurse smiled and patted her arm. "I know, dear. You must feel like you've been trampled by a herd of wild elephants."

Jessica twisted her lips. "Uh-huh. Something like that."

"You just relax, dear. I can give you something for the pain. You're just lucky to be in one piece. Not a single broken bone, and no serious burns, despite being hit with that beam, except for your hand, but that should heal nicely."

The nurse hovered over Jessica again, this time thrusting a thermometer under her tongue. "You've suffered from a bit of smoke inhalation, and probably a bad concussion, but the paramedics on the scene had you quickly stabilized. Now that you are awake and alert, I think you will mend up just fine."

Jessica groaned again. She didn't feel fine. Not without Nate at her side.

The nurse just smiled in encouragement. "I know you feel pretty banged up, but believe me, it could have been a lot worse. The way I hear it, that young man who just left saved your life."

"Nate?" Jessica struggled to remember what had happened after the beam fell on her, but came up blank. The last thing she remembered was looking into Nate's panicked eyes and thinking that was the last thing she was ever going to see.

She had reached for him, and then…

Nothing.

"Do you know what happened?" she asked, her heart fluttering with more than curiosity. Had Nate risked his own life for hers?

"Well, I don't know all the details," the nurse chatted conversationally, waving her arms as she spoke. "What I heard was that your young man ignored the direction of the firefighters and wouldn't leave the building until you were safe. He pulled the beam off you single-handedly, I believe they said."

"Oh, my," Jessica breathed. "And he wasn't hurt?"

The nurse shook her head. "Not so far as I know. A real hero, that one is."

"Yes, he is," Jessica agreed around the lump growing in her throat. It wasn't smoke inhalation making her throat burn now.

The nurse continued to speak as she administered pain medication through Jessica's IV, but the medicine made her instantly groggy and she found it hard to follow the nurse's random, yet comforting chatter. She was only half aware of the doctor checking her over, and cringed only slightly when he shined a penlight directly into her eyes.

"Your pupils are reacting normally," the doctor briskly informed her.

She stared up at him, waiting for him to explain what that meant, and wondering when Nate would come back and see her again.

"That is very good news for you," the doctor

continued. "I think the worst of your injuries are the burn on your hand, some bumps and bruises, and minor smoke inhalation. Your condition is no longer critical, so we'll be moving you down to the third floor. I'm going to keep you here one more night just to be certain, but if all goes well, we can release you tomorrow morning. I'll write you a prescription for some painkillers to take along with you."

Painkillers were the last thing on Jessica's mind. Her head was foggy from this latest round of meds, and now more than ever she wanted to be thinking clearly, not be in a medicated daze.

How was she going to tell Nate what was in her heart if she couldn't even form the words in her head?

She half dozed as the orderlies moved her from one room to another, but she was instantly alert when Nate came into the room.

"Are you up for some company?"

Jessica smiled until her face hurt when Nate entered the room carrying Gracie in his arms. When the baby saw Jessica, she giggled and flapped her arms.

"Take it easy, baby girl," Nate said with a laugh. "Jess can't hold you right now. She has enough bruises for one day, thank you very much."

Jessica's arms ached to hold Gracie and smell her sweet baby smell, but she knew Nate was right. She wasn't strong enough right now to keep a wiggly baby safe in her arms, no matter how much her heart wanted Gracie near.

"She's sure happy to see you," Nate commented, chuckling again. "As well she should be, since you saved her life."

Jessica knew her cheeks were stained with color

from the wave of sudden shyness that overtook her. She didn't know how to handle Nate's compliments, and it unsettled her more than she cared to admit.

Nate moved to the edge of the bed and carefully propped himself on his hip, allowing Jessica to be near Gracie without having to strain herself to hold the baby.

"I admire you so much," he said, his voice low and rough and his gold-flecked green eyes glowing. "You didn't just save Gracie's life, Jess. You saved all those other little kids, too. If it weren't for you dashing head-first into that burning building, who knows how things would have turned out."

His gaze narrowed on her. "Although, to be honest, at the moment, I wanted to throttle you for risking your own life that way."

Jessica reached for Nate's hand and squeezed it with all her remaining strength. "The way I hear it, you're the hero."

Nate immediately shook his head in denial, but Jessica pushed her point.

"Deny it all you want, Mr. Tough Guy Marine," she said, and chuckled. "I'm still going to say it. Thank you for saving my life."

He shook his head once again. "It was nothing. Really. I'm just glad you're okay. What did the doctor say?" he continued in an obvious diversion tactic, meant to take the heat off him.

"The doctor says I'll probably be able to go home tomorrow," she informed him. "And I can't wait to get back home. I hate hospitals."

"Me, too," Nate agreed. "But are you sure you'll

be ready to go back home by tomorrow? How are you going to take care of yourself?"

Jessica barked out a laugh at Nate's obvious distress. "The way I always have. I've suffered more than a few bruises in my lifetime."

Nate brushed her cheek with his palm and stared deep into her eyes.

"More than your share," he whispered, his ragged voice frayed at the ends.

She shook her head, ignoring the throbbing pain. "I have no cause to complain."

"Oh, Jess," he murmured, leaning closer. "I don't know how I would have handled it if you had been seriously injured."

Her heart hammered in her head, replacing the throbbing headache with a new sensation. She tried to swallow, but her throat was too dry and scratchy. She hesitated with the question poised on the tip of her tongue, but at length she could stand it no longer.

"Why?" she inquired softly, half afraid to hear the answer but needing to know just the same.

Nate's gaze swept away from her and focused somewhere out the window, which was telling in itself. There was nothing to view except the stark windows and brick exterior of another wing of Our Lady of Mercy Hospital. He bit his bottom lip reflectively.

Jessica immediately regretted asking the question, and would have wished it away if she could have. She had obviously embarrassed him by putting him on the spot. She should have known he didn't necessarily reciprocate the depth of what she felt for him. She certainly shouldn't have pushed him. She had no right.

Nate was enough of a gentleman not to want to

hurt her when she was down, and he clearly didn't know how to answer her abrupt question. How had she not realized what she was doing to him? The medicine must have addled her brain more than she had realized.

Heat flooded to her face as she searched for something to say that would effectively take Nate off the grandstand she'd placed him on. She would say anything if it would return the smile to his face.

After a long moment of silence, Nate's gaze returned to hers. His eyes appeared shiny and glassy, and he shrugged as if apologizing for taking his time.

She shook her head, trying to figure out a way to apologize for putting him on the spot.

"I don't know if now is the right time," he began, then cleared his throat over his rough voice. "But I have to speak."

Jessica held her breath, waiting for him to continue, expecting he would try to let her down easy, given the circumstances.

"I cannot imagine where Gracie and I would be without you," he said, his voice still filled with gravel. "If you hadn't shown up in our lives when you did, who knows whether or not I could have coped with becoming a new father."

"You would have done fine," she assured him, her throat so dry she could barely speak. Tears pricked at the backs of her eyes. "You love Gracie. You would have found a way."

"I'm not so sure about that," he replied, shaking his head. "Either way, though, it would have been a lot rougher a ride for me without your encouragement."

"I'm glad I could help," she said, and she knew it

was true. Whatever Nate was trying to get at, and even if her heart was about to be broken once again, she could never regret the time she had spent with Nate and Gracie. She would treasure those memories forever.

His gaze captured hers. "I guess you already know I'm in love with you."

Her sudden intake of breath was audible to both of them, and her hands were trembling.

"I'm sorry," he apologized immediately. "I knew I should have waited until later to say something, until you've had more time to recuperate. I'm an insensitive oaf."

"You," Jessica argued softly, "are the kindest, most patient, most wonderful man in the whole world."

Hope flamed from his eyes as he reached for her hand and held it gently. He didn't speak for a moment as he stared down at their interlocked fingers.

"When you ran into the blaze to save the children, I thought my world might end. I didn't know what I would do if I lost you."

"But you didn't."

"No. And to my great surprise, I was never alone, not even when I didn't know if you and Gracie were going to be okay."

His gaze beamed even brighter. What was he trying to tell her?

"God was there," he said simply.

She squeezed his hand, joy flooding through her at his admission. "I'm glad."

"Me, too," he agreed. "More than you know."

He paused, pursing his lips as he considered his next words.

"Jess?" he asked softly.

"Yes?" Her heart was roaring in her ears so loudly that she wasn't certain she'd be able to hear him when he spoke.

"I know you've been through a lot, both in your past, and now with the fire. You've suffered pain and loss that I've only had a glimpse of, but somehow I think that is part of what makes you the strong, vibrant woman I see before me now."

"Oh, Nate," she breathed.

"You're the kind of woman I never even dared to dream about," he continued. "I never expected to find the love of my life, especially not coming home to Morningway Lodge, which always held bad memories for me.

"But I did. I found you. I love you. And I want to make you happy."

"You do," she assured him.

He leaned in closer, so that his face was only inches from hers. Baby Gracie was still cuddled into his chest, but she didn't add distance between them; rather, she seemed to complete the little circle of their love. "Will you be my wife?"

She couldn't speak, and stared at him wide-eyed and trembling.

"I know that's asking a lot from you. I come with strings attached. Marrying me means becoming Gracie's mother. But I know Gracie loves you as much as I do. Please say you'll make our family complete. Can you see us as part of your future?"

Jessica brushed her palm across Nate's cheek. Even with her commitment phobia, she could not deny the love in his eyes, nor the answering beat of her own heart.

"You and Gracie *are* my future," she whispered raggedly. "And I can't imagine anything that would give me greater joy than to be your wife and Gracie's mama."

"Ma-ma-ma-ma-ma," Gracie squealed, patting Jessica and Nate on the head simultaneously.

They both laughed. Ignoring her body aches, the IV drip and her bandaged hand, she wrapped her arms around Nate and the baby and tipped her chin up to receive Nate's gentle, bargain-sealing kiss.

God was good, all the time. He had known the desire of Jessica's heart before she even knew herself, and had blessed her with a hope and a future that she never would have imagined.

"My family." She said the words aloud, wondering how one human being could experience as much joy as was flooding from her heart at that moment. "God has blessed me with a family."

The next day, while the doctor signed Jess's release papers, Nate stepped out of the room to call his brother to inform him of his plans.

"Vince," Nate said when his brother picked up the line. "Jess is being released from the hospital today. I was wondering if you could meet us at her cabin to help her get settled in?"

"Of course," Vince answered immediately. "How is she doing?"

"Better," Nate assured him. "But she has to rest and recuperate for a while before she'll be all the way back to normal."

"I imagine so."

"Meet us at Jess's cabin in an hour and a half?" Nate queried.

"You got it, bro."

Nate clicked his cell phone off and stuffed it in his jacket pocket, but he didn't immediately return to Jess's room. He closed his eyes, savoring the excitement of the moment.

He and Jess hadn't yet told anyone of their engagement. Vince would be the first to know. And for some reason Nate didn't really understand, he couldn't wait to share his good news with his brother.

Up until the day of the fire, Vince would have been the last person Nate would want to share good news with. There was still a niggling of doubt in his mind of whether or not Vince would approve of the engagement, and an even bigger uncertainty as to why that mattered one way or the other.

Why did he care what Vince thought?

But he did. Something had changed between him and his brother. It was small, but it was a start to rebuilding a relationship with him.

At least, that was what Nate hoped.

It was another half an hour before Nate had Jess strapped into his Jeep for the drive back up to Morningway Lodge. The road was bumpy even before they hit the washboard dirt, and Nate worried for Jess's comfort. Out of his peripheral vision, he saw her clench her jaw a few times, but she never complained aloud.

Still, she was looking fatigued by the time they reached her cabin. Vince's SUV was parked in front, and he was leaning against the hood, waiting. As soon as Nate parked the Jeep, Vince moved to the passenger door to help Jess out of the vehicle.

"Are you sure she should be out of the hospital already?" Vince asked Nate over Jess's head.

"*She* can hear you," Jess complained playfully. "And trust me, I'm going to get a lot more rest in my own bed than I did at the hospital."

Vince scowled. "I still don't like the idea of her—you—being alone up here."

"She won't be alone," Nate assured him, swiftly unbuckling Gracie from her car seat and lifting her into his arms.

"I can check with the Rocky Mountain Rehabilitation Hospital to see if they have any nurses available. At least for the first few days."

Nate flashed his brother a wide grin. "Not necessary, bro."

"I just think that—"

Nate held up his hand to stop Vince's flow of words. "You're going to have to put up with my presence here at Morningway Lodge for a little longer, I'm afraid."

Vince looked flustered. He shook his head. "You're welcome to stay on here. The lodge is your home as much as it is mine."

Nate smiled at the unexpectedly welcome tone in Vince's voice. "I'm glad to hear it. This may be permanent."

"Yeah?" Vince asked.

"Yeah," Nate agreed. "I'll personally see to it that Jess isn't left alone, and that she rests up according to the doctor's orders. Believe me, no one is more worried about the health of my future wife than I am."

His grin widened at Jess's surprised gasp of breath and the way Vince took a literal step backward, as if someone had punched him.

"Your *what?*" Vince squawked, looking between Nate and Jess in disbelief. "Did I hear you right?"

Nate experienced one brief moment of uncertainty about Vince's reaction, but he quickly brushed it off.

Did he really care how Vince took the news? Nate was marrying the most wonderful woman in the world. Life didn't get any better than this, and Nate was going to enjoy every moment of it.

"Jess has agreed to become my wife," Nate announced, moving to Jess's other side and draping his arm across her shoulder.

Her answering smile meant everything to him.

"Seriously?" Vince asked, his voice rising to an unusually high pitch.

Jess's smile didn't change, nor did the love flowing from her eyes, but Nate felt her shoulders tense under his arm.

To his surprise, she winked at him before turning to Vince. "Seriously."

"W-well, then," Vince stammered. It was the first time Nate could remember seeing his brother lose his self-possession. He waited, holding his breath, to find out whether that was a good thing or a bad thing.

"I see," Vince continued, his expression still deadly serious. "You're sure about this? Hitching yourself up to this fellow?"

Jess beamed. "More sure than I've ever been about anything in my whole life."

"Even though he has a baby?"

"*Especially* because he has a baby," she assured him with a laugh. "Who could resist this gruff marine when he's holding that cute little baby girl in his arms?"

Vince pressed his free hand to his hip and cocked

his head to one side, sizing Nate up as if considering whether or not Jess's words were true.

Nate stared at the pair, speechless, feeling as if he were a zoo animal on display.

Suddenly, Vince's face split into a grin. "You've got a point there."

"Of course I do." She wrapped her arm around Nate's waist and squeezed him hard, then winked at Vince. "Honestly, I couldn't possibly love your brother more than I do. And I love Gracie as if she was my own daughter."

Her eyes misted, but only for a moment, and then she smiled radiantly.

Vince shrugged and chuckled. "In that case, let me be the first to welcome you to the family."

He leaned down and pressed a kiss to Jess's cheek, then reached around her to slap Nate on the back. "Well done, little brother."

"I'll say," he agreed, pulling Jess even closer against him. With Gracie in one arm and Jess in the other, he turned them all toward Jess's cabin.

"Come on, now," he murmured, his heart welling with so much love he wondered how he could bear the weight of it. "Let's go home."

* * * * *

Dear Reader,

Thank you for sharing in Nate and Jessica's journey at Morningway Lodge with me. As Nate and Jessica discovered, we can always depend on God. He is ever-present and unchanging.

Are you facing a tough period in your life, or are you desperate to put the past behind you? It is my prayer that you will discover God's loving presence in whatever part of the journey you currently find yourself.

I always appreciate hearing from my readers and try to respond personally to everyone. I can be reached by e-mail at DEBWRTR@aol.com, or look me up on Facebook. I look forward to hearing from you!

By Him and In Him and Through Him,

Deb Kastner

QUESTIONS FOR DISCUSSION

1. Throughout the story, Nate struggles with feeling he has let everyone in his life down, including God. Have you ever felt this way? Can we earn God's love?

2. Jessica built a fortress around her heart because she was afraid to be hurt by losing someone again. How did this affect her relationship with Nate? With God?

3. What are the major themes of this novel? Which one strikes closest to your heart?

4. Jessica lost her baby to SIDS. Do you know anyone who has recently lost someone to illness or accident? How can you extend God's love to this person?

5. Nate is raising his best friend's baby as his own. Would you raise someone else's child?

6. Nate is a fixer. He doesn't want to pray, he wants to act. But sometimes the most powerful thing we can do is pray. Describe a situation in your life where the power of prayer was your most valuable weapon.

7. Which character do you most identify with? Why?

8. It was Jessica's witness of her own tragedy that led Nate to a better understanding of his relationship with God. How can you use the trials you've endured to witness Christ's love to others?

9. Nate has a strained relationship with his brother Vince. What, if anything, do you think he can do to bridge the gap between them?

10. Morningway Lodge is a retreat from everyday life, a quiet place for people to go and reconnect with God. Is there a special place you like to go to fill up your spiritual tank?

11. Nate finally realized God loved him, not for anything Nate had done, but despite it. Do you recognize God's unconditional love for you?

12. Even though she risked her own heart, Jessica selflessly gave of her time and attention when Nate and Gracie needed her most. Has someone ever done that for you?

13. Nate wants to be in control of his life. It is only when he realizes he is not that his relationship with God can grow. What areas of your life do you need to hand over to God?

14. Jessica lives in fear that the past will repeat itself. How can she conquer her fear?

15. What do you think of Nate and Jessica as a couple? Do they belong together?

**The mission trip to Mexico was supposed to be an
adventure. But the thrill turns sour when Jenna Dougherty
and her roommate Magdalena are kidnapped.**

"It's okay. I'm here to help." The voice was as deep as the
darkness, but Jenna Dougherty didn't believe the lie. She
could do nothing but lie still as hands slid down her arms,
felt the rope around her wrists.

"I'm going to use a knife to cut you free, Jenna. Hold
still."

The cold blade of a knife pressed close to her head before
her gag fell away.

"I—" she started, but her mouth was dry, and she could
do nothing but suck in air.

"Shhh. Whatever needs to be said can be said when
we're out of here." Nick spoke quietly, his hand gentle on
her cheek. There and gone as he sliced through the ropes on
her wrists and ankles.

He pulled her upright. "Come on. We may be on
borrowed time."

"I can't leave my friend," Jenna rasped out.

"There's no one here. Just us."

"She has to be here." Jenna took a step away.

"There's no one here. Let's go before that changes."

"It's dark. Maybe if we find a light…"

"What did you say?"

"We need to turn on the light. I can't leave until I know that—"

"What can you see, Jenna?"

"Nothing."

"No shadows? No light?"

"No."

"It's broad daylight. There's light spilling in from the window I climbed in through. You can't see it?"

She went cold at his words.

"I can't see anything."

"You've got a nasty bruise on your forehead. Maybe that has something to do with it." His fingers traced the tender flesh on her forehead.

"It doesn't matter *how* it happened. I'm blind!"

Can Nick help Jenna find her friend or will chasing this trail have Jenna running blindly again into danger?

Find out in RUNNING BLIND, available in November 2010 only from Love Inspired Suspense.